He lay outside on the front veranda of the neat suburban house. Blood was a halo around his head, a cloak spread beneath his shoulders, a sticky darkening stain that had dyed the front of his white T-shirt and splattered down his jeans. Even the soles of his worn tennis shoes were covered with blood...

It was a beautiful spring day, sunny, yet still with a touch of bracing coolness. A sparrow hopped onto the veranda railing and cocked its head inquisitively. Detective Inspector Carol Ashton stood staring down into the face of her friend. Steve's blue eyes were wide with surprise, not horror...

"However long it takes, Steve," she said softly. "However long it takes."

CHAIN LETTER

THE 9TH A DETECTIVE INSPECTOR CAROL ASHTON MYSTERY

CLAIRE McNAB

THE NAIAD PRESS, INC.
1997

Printed in the United States of America on acid-free paper
First Edition

Editor: Lila Empson
Cover designer: Bonnie Liss (Phoenix Graphics)
Typesetter: Sandi Stancil

Library of Congress Cataloging-in-Publication Data

McNab, Claire.
    Chain letter : a Carol Ashton mystery / by Claire McNab.
        p.   cm.
    ISBN 1-56280-181-3 (pbk.)
    1. Ashton, Carol (Fictitious character)—Fiction.   I. Title.
PS3563.C3877C48   1997
813'.54—dc21   97-10008
                                                                         CIP

For Sheila

ACKNOWLEDGMENTS

My deepest thanks to my editor, Lila Empson, for her admirable editing under trying circumstances; and to Sandi Stancil, who has, singlehanded, proved herself a wonder woman.

ABOUT THE AUTHOR

CLAIRE McNAB is the author of nine Detective
Inspector Carol Ashton mysteries: *Lessons in Murder,*
Fatal Reunion, Death Down Under, Cop Out, Dead
Certain, Body Guard, Double Bluff, Inner Circle and
Chain Letter. She has also written two romances,
Under the Southern Cross and *Silent Heart.*

In her native Australia she is known for her
crime fiction, plays, children's novels and self-help
books.

Now permanently resident in Los Angeles, Claire
teaches fiction writing in the UCLA Extension
Writers' Program. She makes it a point to return to
Australia once a year to refresh her Aussie accent.

PROLOGUE

TO WHOM IT MAY CONCERN

For they have sown the wind, and they shall reap the whirlwind.

You are a chosen one. Your name has been selected to receive these instructions.

Follow them exactly and you will have great good fortune. Fail, and this letter will bring you death.

Do not break the chain.

1

Within forty-eight hours you must copy this letter and send it anonymously to ten other people. Wonderful things will begin to happen for you within two weeks.

If you do not do this, you will die.

You have forty-eight hours. Do not break the chain.

CHAPTER ONE

There was blood everywhere in the hallway. Red splashed the cream walls, pooled on the parquet floor. Several lines of fine drops had sprayed the pale ceiling. The edge of the door and the handle were smeared with it.

He lay outside on the front veranda of the neat suburban house. Blood was a halo around his head, a cloak spread beneath his shoulders, a sticky darkening stain that had dyed the front of his white T-shirt and splattered down his jeans. Even the soles of his worn tennis shoes were covered with blood.

Crimson impatiens in wooden half-barrels on either side of the stone steps leading up from the garden echoed the color.

It was a beautiful spring day, sunny, yet still with a touch of bracing coolness. A sparrow hopped onto the veranda railing and cocked its head inquisitively. Detective Inspector Carol Ashton stood staring down into the face of her friend. She ignored the bustle of technicians around her. Steve's blue eyes were wide with surprise, not horror. He had been stabbed repeatedly, fatally, yet his expression was tranquil, his bloody hands relaxed.

Liz Carey, head of the crime-scene team, came to stand beside her. "It still amazes me," she said.

Carol took a deep breath, consciously pushing her grief to one side and assuming her professional role of investigating officer. "What does?"

Liz gestured with a gloved hand. "That peaceful expression, after what's been done to him. I've seen it before, particularly in children who've died in sudden, unexpected violence. Maybe it's that everything happens so quickly. And he died fast." She indicated a deep cut in his throat. "Looks like the carotid artery's gone. From that moment, he probably had a minute, tops."

Carol turned her gaze back to Steve's face. There was a superficial slash across one cheek, and blood had bubbled out of his mouth to stiffen the new mustache he had recently begun to cultivate. She remembered the good-natured ribbing he'd endured about his facial hair last night when they'd all gathered in a pub for after-work drinks.

She looked up as Detective Sergeant Bourke took the veranda steps two at a time. He halted beside

4

them. "Jesus. It *is* Steve. "When I heard the address, I hoped . . ." He let his breath out with a long sigh. "Anyone told Lauren?'

"Not yet. Would you do that, Mark?"

Unconsciously, he put up his hands and tugged at his cropped brown hair. "Carol . . . they were getting married next week . . . I was going to be the best man . . ."

"Would you rather a stranger told her?"

Her cold voice had the desired effect. He dropped his hands and straightened his shoulders. "Of course not. I'll do it right now. And I'll call Pat, so Lauren will have someone with her." Bourke bent his head. "Jesus, Steve," he said, almost as if blaming the dead man for the situation.

Liz glanced at him dispassionately, then said to Carol, "Come inside. Now that they've pretty well finished with the immediate crime scene, there're a couple of things you'll want to see."

They stepped around the puddles of congealing blood, obscenely incongruous on the highly polished parquet floor. "Nice," said Liz, looking around. "Really done the place up."

Carol thought of the wedding that now would not take place, and how they'd all been joking at work about Steve's nesting complex and the painstaking steps he'd been taking to make the shabby house he'd bought into a perfect home.

"All right, Liz, what do you want to show me?" She made sure her tone was matter-of-fact. Whatever she felt personally, no emotions were going to affect the smooth running of this investigation.

"There's no blood anywhere else in the house, and I figure he was first attacked here, in the hallway.

Look here . . ." Liz indicated an area on the floor two meters in from the front door. "See that semicircular mark in the blood next to the footprint? It matches the blood on the right knee of his jeans. And here?" She pointed to a slide mark closer to the door. "He steps into his own blood, and slips."

Liz tilted her head as she surveyed the scene. "I reckon he was stabbed several times, maybe in the throat and chest, and blood gushed out of him onto the floor. He goes down on one knee." She flicked a finger at the wall. "That smear shows where he steadied himself with his right hand. Then he got to his feet."

Carol could see it all, as though she were an unwilling witness. One moment Steve was alive, vital — the next he was mortally wounded, his blood pumping from his body as he turned and tried to escape. Had he realized, in those last moments, that everything for him was over?

Liz was pointing to the ceiling. "Those fine spray lines came from the murder weapon, already covered in blood." She mimicked stabbing motions, the imaginary knife lifted high to plunge down into an invisible victim. "Every time the perp raised the weapon, he sent a spray of blood clear to the ceiling." She gave a dry smile. "Got quite carried away, he did."

"Did you notice any defense wounds on the victim's hands?"

Carol heard herself refer to Steve as a victim with a pang. If Steve could hear her, he'd understand. There had to be distance between them. He was no longer a colleague, a friend, but the object of a fatal attack. She blinked as she felt tears prick her eyes. *Toughen up!* she snarled to herself.

"A few cuts on his hands," Liz was saying. "Nothing particularly deep. I think he was taken by complete surprise and hardly had time to try to defend himself. He just tried to get away."

"Any evidence of forced entry?"

"No, but the back door's unlocked, and most of the windows are open. Some of the rooms are freshly painted, so he was obviously airing out the house."

"Is there a back entrance?"

"Yes, a lane runs behind all these houses in the block. There's a separate garage and a back gate. It's just got a latch, so anyone could walk right in."

Carol looked at the polished floor running away to the back of the house. "Why isn't there blood somewhere else? The person who did this must have been drenched."

Pleased at the question, Liz indicated a series of semicircular drop patterns near the doorway to the front room. "Exactly. There's no way you could avoid getting blood on you. I'm guessing here, and the blood evidence expert will have a better opinion, but I'd say he was wearing something to protect his clothes, like a plastic raincoat. He took it off, gave it a shake or two to get rid of some of the blood, then folded it up and took it with him."

He, thought Carol. *This has to be a man.* But then, she had known women who had killed with knives, stabbing over and over again . . .

"Inspector?" It was a uniformed patrol officer. "We've got the gardener sitting in the car. Do you want to see him?"

Carol nodded to her, then said to Liz, "I want this house completely processed — every room and every item. I want an analysis of everything, down to the finest detail. The same outside to beyond the boundaries, especially at the back."

Liz raised her eyebrows. "That'll take some time."

"Do it."

Carol turned to the officer. "What's the gardener's name?"

"His name's Joe Silvano. He was working in the front here when it happened. He's the one who gave the alarm."

Carol followed her down the front steps, past the red impatiens in their brown barrels, and into the front garden. A freshly-painted white picket fence enclosed a rectangle of recently-mowed lawn edged by hydrangea bushes and freshly-turned flower beds.

Crime-scene tape and the admonitions of two patrol officers held back the cluster of people who always seemed to materialize at crime scenes. Carol had often wondered if they were summoned by some strange group-sense of disaster, some bush telegraph that signaled violence and murder.

The middle-aged man clambered out of the backseat as soon as he saw Carol approaching. He was white faced and shaking, and leaned against the open patrol car door as if for support. He seemed unaware of the blood soaked into his faded green T-shirt and grubby khaki shorts, or the streaks of dried blood on his hands.

"Mr. Silvano?"

"Are you in charge? I need to talk to the person in charge." His voice still had a touch of an accent.

Carol introduced herself. He disregarded her

8

invitation to sit down, but nodded, distracted, then the words spilled out of him.

"I was just doing the garden for him, that's all. Working Sunday to do something extra, so it'd be ready for the wedding. The sarge said he had a black thumb, you know? He was doing up the house, could handle everything else pretty much, but he needed me for the garden, here and at the back. I'd mowed the lawn, was just doing the flower beds, when I heard this sound. Sort of . . ."

He raised his open hands, stiff fingered. "Sort of like a wet shout. And I turned round, and I saw him . . ." The man pointed with a tremulous hand. "Up there. I saw the blood on his T-shirt, and then he fell down . . ."

"Did you see who attacked Sergeant York?"

Silvano stared at her, as if this were a new thought that the murderer had still been there. "No. I didn't see anyone. Just the sarge."

Carol took his arm and led him through the impeccably white front gate into the garden. "Please show me where you were working."

The crowd surged against the tape, confident that something interesting was happening. "It's that Carol Ashton," said someone loudly.

"She looks much better on TV," said someone else disparagingly. "What in hell's she done to her nose?"

Carol resisted the impulse to touch her face. Her black eyes and most of the bruising had faded, but her nose, smashed by a rifle butt, had remained obstinately swollen, even after corrective plastic surgery.

Silvano pointed to a heavy spade, discarded on the grass near a hydrangea bush laden with heavy white

9

and purple clusters. "Right over there. Had my back to the house, digging, and then I heard something, and turned around . . ." His face folded into lines of pain. "It was awful."

Carol nodded sympathetically. "I know this is hard for you, Mr. Silvano."

"Yeah, well . . ." He swallowed. "I got up there, fast as I could. Didn't even think that there might be someone still in the house." Silvano looked up at the veranda and the half-open front door. "I never gave it a thought . . ."

"Please tell me exactly what happened." Carol gestured at the stairs. "You're digging here, you hear something, turn around. You realize there's something wrong with Sergeant York, and you go up the stairs. And then?"

"He was on his back, and there was so much blood. It was just pouring out of him. I had to do something. I shouted for help, then I got down on my knees, lifted him up, tried to stop the bleeding, but I knew it was hopeless."

"Did he say anything?"

"There was blood in his mouth — I don't think he could speak. Some people came running up the stairs . . ." He gestured vaguely. "Neighbors. I said to get an ambulance."

Carol looked to the officer, standing attentively nearby, who nodded at the unspoken question. "We have their names."

Silvano was still speaking. "I kept on telling him he'd be okay — I didn't know what else to do. He was staring at me and taking huge breaths, like he couldn't get enough air. Then he fell back in my arms, and . . ." He raised his shoulders helplessly.

The man's eyes filled with tears. "He was a good bloke, you know. Maybe I could have done more . . ."

"You did everything you could." She waited until he had regained composure, then said, "Did you hear any movement in the house?"

"No."

"Perhaps you looked into the hallway through the front door."

"All I saw was the sarge." His glance fell to his hands, and he examined them, gazing at the dried blood under his fingernails. "When he stopped breathing, I should have done something. But his mouth was full of blood."

Carol steered him back toward the patrol car. "There was nothing you could do. He was beyond help."

She mouthed the platitudes in a soothing voice, giving no hint of the grief and outrage she felt. Why did Steve York — a fine person and admirable police officer — have to lie dying in pools of his own blood?

"Mr. Silvano, I'm afraid we have to ask you to give a full written statement."

The gardener turned toward her. "Who could have done this dreadful thing?"

"I don't know, but we'll find out." Carol said this with every confidence. When it was one of their own, the police service would provide every resource for as long as it took. No matter how much time passed, there was no such thing as an inactive designation for a cop killing.

Silvano backed into the backseat, and sat slumped with his feet outside on the grass verge. "The sarge was such a good bloke. Why would anyone want to kill him?"

11

Carol didn't answer. What could she say that would mean anything? There were many people who had reason to hate the police, and some might be motivated to violence — but this was the frenzied attack of someone mad with fear or rage.

She turned at the slam of a car door. The medical examiner had arrived. He half-saluted her as he hurried through the gate in the picket fence. Carol watched him climb the stone steps — steps up which Steve had vowed he'd ceremoniously carry Lauren after their wedding. It had been a standing joke at work, with much laughing comment about the body-building gym time Steve would need to do to accomplish his pledge.

"However long it takes, Steve," she said softly. "However long it takes."

CHAPTER TWO

Carol had walked up and down the rear lane, and peered into adjacent backyards. Now she came back out into the nondescript suburban street. The grass verge on either side was lined with oleander bushes flowering in shades of pink or red.

The crush of onlookers had grown, and Carol's appearance caused a buzz of excitement. A reporter with a television crew in tow ducked under the tape and dodged around an officer on crowd control. "Inspector Ashton! A statement?"

Carol gave a slight negative shake of her head,

accompanied by a moderate expression of regret. She respected the power of the media and worked them as assiduously as they worked her.

Turning her back on the crowd and ignoring the comments and questions, she concentrated on the row of houses before her. Steve's was like all the others, dwellings built in the forties and fifties in the postwar boom. They were undistinguished single-story brick buildings with red tile roofs, each sitting isolated on its own rectangular block of land, the boundaries clearly delineated with paling fences on three sides and a choice of brick or wooden fences along the front. Flowers brightened most front areas, and vegetable gardens, many with the ubiquitous choko or passionfruit vines smothering the nearest fence, bordered the back lawns. Almost all had a single-car garage at the rear, although many of these had been converted into double carports.

The gardener's calls had brought help from Steve's neighbors on Carol's right — the neighbors on the other side had been at church. Carol paused at the front gate. The garden was neat enough, but the front fence sagged, apparently being held up by a series of small flowering bushes. The redbrick house was bluffly unadorned, and the cream woodwork needed a coat of paint. Like Steve's, a short flight of stone steps led to a small veranda and the front door.

Stopping halfway up the steps, Carol looked over at Steve's house. From this angle she couldn't see the veranda, but his front garden and steps were in clear view. She could imagine Mr. Silvano's cries splitting the quiet Sunday morning, people putting down their papers, saying to each other, "What was that?"

14

Inside, Anne Newsome, her buoyant physicality in check, was sitting demurely at the kitchen table. The constable stood as Carol entered the faded kitchen. "This is Mr. Edward Parcell, Inspector."

Carol shook the seated man's hand. His grip was surprisingly firm. Although he was old, perhaps in his late eighties, and frail, with skin blotched and papery, he still gave an impression of stubborn vigor, and his pale blue eyes were sharp.

"I'm Inspector Ashton," she said.

He nodded, his almost hairless skull bobbing dangerously on his thin, corded neck. "Yeah, I seen you on the telly."

Carol slid onto a hard, straight-back wooden chair. The kitchen was very clean and tidy, but the surface of the sturdy unpainted table at which she sat had been scrubbed so often that its surface was full of dips and hollows, the edge of the old porcelain sink was chipped, and the cracked linoleum on the floor had almost lost its original intricate pattern of squares and circles.

She glanced over at Constable Newsome, who had seated herself again and opened a notebook. Anne was a conscientious note-taker, something she had learned from Mark Bourke. Now she sat with pen poised, ready to record any and all details. Carol thought of all the notebooks she, herself, had filled over the years with information that was very often useless — but sometimes those scribbled notations held the key to a mystery.

Carol turned her attention to the old man, who was watching her intently. "Can you tell me what happened, Mr. Parcell?"

"I reckon I can," he said. "Me and the missus, we

15

were having a cup of tea right here in the kitchen" — he paused to indicate an ancient brown teapot, two cups and saucers both nearly full with obviously cold milky liquid, and a plate of iced biscuits — "when we heard a bit of a commotion next door. I went to see what was up, and Marge came too."

Carol looked around. "Is your wife here?"

This question amused him mightily. "After what's happened? She's out bending the ear of anyone who'll listen. Best story she's had for years."

Carol sighed to herself. Apart from possible contamination of other witnesses, some of the ears Marge Parcell would be bending no doubt belonged to the media.

"What exactly did you hear?" she asked.

"The dago bloke, he yells out."

"Mr. Silvano?"

"Yeah. The I-tie. Screaming his head off, he is. We go in, and he's up on the veranda, still yelling." Mr. Parcell pursed his lips and shook his head.

"And?" Carol prompted.

"Well, I don't mind admitting it gave me quite a turn. I was in the army, you know, Second World War, North Africa, so I can take it with the best of 'em, but this was pretty awful. Blood everywhere. Knew right away he was a goner."

"Did you see a knife or any weapon?"

"No, nothin'."

He leaned forward, propping his sharp elbows on the table, his pale eyes narrowed. "You thinking the I-tie did it, are you? Barking up the wrong tree, if you do. When I came down the side of the house, I looked over and seen him digging in the garden.

Then Marge calls me to say the tea's ready. I come in, quick smart, and I haven't had but one bite of biscuit and a swallow of tea, before he starts screaming his head off."

"So, as soon as you heard Mr. Silvano shouting, you and your wife immediately went next door?"

"Didn't hang around — he was screaming blue murder."

"You went up on the veranda, took a look, and went straight for help. Is that right?"

He gave Carol an irritated frown. "Course. Told Marge to stay there, case she could do anything — though I knew she couldn't — and went for the phone."

"The phone in Sergeant York's house?"

Parcell looked affronted, as though Carol were accusing him of some misdeed. "Well, it was an emergency, wasn't it? And he wasn't going to complain, take my word for it." A slight smile twisted his skinny lips. "Worried I might have tramped in the blood, are you? Well, I didn't. I was careful."

"After you made the call, did you look through the house at all?"

He gave a bark of laughter. "Cripes, woman, I'm not that stupid. Got the hell out. If someone was there with a knife, I didn't want to meet him."

Carol saw Anne hide a smile. A little amused herself, she said, "That was wise, Mr. Parcell."

He nodded agreement. "Too right."

"Did you know Sergeant York well?"

"Good bloke. He was fixing up the place, wanted it just right before he got hitched. I helped him with a few things — always been good with my hands.

17

Matter of fact, just seen the sarge this morning, out the back. Had a bit of a yak over the fence."

He leaned back, thoughtful. "You know, he told me he was waiting for an exterminator. Said the bloke was going to check under the house for white ants. Said it was for free, so I said to the sarge, if it's free, tell him to pop over here when he's finished with you."

Not letting her sudden keen interest show, Carol said, "And did the exterminator come to your house?"

"Didn't see hide nor hair of him."

"Did you ever see this person, even at a distance?"

"Can't say I did."

She leaned forward, willing him to know something — anything. "Do you know the name of the exterminator company?"

Parcell rested his chin on his bony hands. "None of the biggies. Some little fly-by-night show with a fancy moniker. The van was parked in the lane a couple of times. White, it was, with red lettering on the side. Fresh, like it'd just been done — beautiful job, actually." He furrowed his brow. "I just can't remember the name. Marge might."

Marge, when she came home for a break from gossiping, certainly did.

"Real funny," she said. "Like a joke, you know? Called himself *Terror of Insects*. It was right there on the van. Bit of a laugh, eh?"

CHAPTER THREE

"There's no such exterminator company listed in the yellow pages," said Anne Newsome as she came into Carol's plain, impersonal office.

Carol put aside yesterday's mail that she'd collected from her mailbox when she'd hurried out of her house at dawn after a few hours of restless sleep. Aunt Sarah's brightly-colored postcard was on top, an enticing underwater view of the tropical fish of the Barrier Reef. With three cronies in a minivan, her aunt was making a leisurely coastal circuit of the entire continent of Australia, visiting national parks.

She was sending postcards to Carol from each place they stopped. They had left Sydney three weeks before, and this was the sixth Carol had received.

"*Terror of Insects* is an unusual name," said Carol. "If the company exists, it should be easy to find."

"I've tried trade associations, insecticide and chemical suppliers, small business groups, and the local paper in Steve's area. No one's ever heard of it." Anne bounced gently on the balls of her feet, radiating health and vitality. "And there was no mailbox drop of flyers in the neighborhood, so it's not just someone starting out who isn't listed anywhere yet."

As always, Carol was careful to hide the indulgent affection she had for the young constable. Anne Newsome reminded Carol of herself when she had been at the beginning of her career. True, Anne's short, curly chestnut hair, brown eyes, and slightly stocky build did not resemble Carol's sleek blond athleticism, but the drive to succeed, the single-minded focus with which she had started her career certainly did.

Anne said, "The guy's a fake."

"He's a murderer."

Carol moved from behind her paper-strewn desk and went to lean against the window frame, where she could look out at the uninspiring neutral wall of the adjoining building or, if she craned her neck, she could catch a glimpse of trees and a busy road.

"I've checked with Liz Carey." she said to Anne. "There was nothing in Steve's house to give us a lead — not a phone number, a brochure, or an extermination quote. And the closest any neighbor came to seeing him was a glimpse of a man in navy overalls. He could be anyone."

When she turned her head, something in Anne Newsome's manner told her the young constable was holding something back. "Okay, Anne, you've got something, haven't you?"

"I got to thinking about Mr. Parcell saying that the lettering on the van was fresh. He said it was a beautiful job, so I presumed it was professionally done."

"You've found the signwriter?"

"Looks like it." She grinned at Carol. "I thought it would take ages, but it was the third one I got from the ads in the yellow pages. The guy remembered *Terror of Insects*. Told me he thought it was a stupid name."

Carol wanted action. She wanted to interview someone who had a face to put on the man who had murdered Steve. "When are you seeing him?"

"This afternoon at four. It's the earliest he's got free time."

The phone on Carol's desk burred. Looking back over her shoulder as she leaned to answer it, Carol said, "I'll go with you."

When she heard Jeff Duke's voice, she waved a dismissal to Anne and moved back behind her desk to sink down into the embrace of her worn leather chair.

The pathologist's hearty voice boomed over the phone. "I'm doing the post on York tomorrow. I knew you'd want me to bump it up the schedule."

"Can you tell me anything?"

"Cause of death was acute hemorrhage leading to hypovolemic shock," said the pathologist. "But you know that already, Carol."

Carol moved to one side some of the papers that had accumulated on her desk and took the cap off her gold pen. "Are there any other details you can give me, Jeff?"

"Multiple stabs wounds, throat, chest, and back, any number of which could have been fatal. Delivered in a frenzy. Probably a two-edged knife of substantial size. He died fast, probably within a few minutes of the initial attack. I'll know more when I do the post-mortem. You going to be there?"

She closed her eyes. She couldn't ask Mark Bourke to attend in her place. He usually hid his feelings behind a pleasantly opaque manner, but she knew him so well, and this murder of a colleague and friend — Mark and his wife, Pat, had been very close to Steve and Lauren — had shaken him deeply.

"When is it scheduled?" She could hear the reluctance in her voice.

He gave an amused snort. "That keen, are you? In that case I'll see you tomorrow, around eleven."

As she replaced the receiver, she thought of the other cases she'd investigated where victims had bled to death. Sometimes they seemed hardly hurt, stabbed once, perhaps, and still alert and talking. But inside, unstoppable bleeding had begun, the blood gushing out an artery — perhaps a nicked aorta — and pooling in the body cavities.

She remembered how, as a young officer, she had watched one young street kid die while ambulance officers fought to keep him alive. He'd been in a knife fight and had been stabbed in the stomach. One moment he was swearing at her, acting tough. The next, his eyes had widened and he had begun to hyperventilate.

She hadn't understood the process then, but by now Carol had witnessed enough postmortems, heard enough dry dissertations from pathologists, to know what happened in a fatal stabbing.

She could almost hear Jeff Duke explaining with his usual gusto: As the volume of blood circulating drops, the victim begins to breathe more quickly in an effort to compensate for falling oxygen levels. For the same reason, the heart beats harder and harder. The loss of blood continues, to the point where the brain ceases to receive enough oxygen. Unconsciousness follows, and shortly thereafter, the heart stops.

Incongruously, an image from her school days rose unbidden in her mind — the sleepwalking Lady Macbeth washing imaginary spots of blood from her hands. Carol smiled wryly, remembering how she had played the part in a billowing white nightgown too long for her, so she was constantly catching her toes in the hem.

She sobered as she remembered Lady Macbeth's words about the king she had incited her husband to butcher, "Yet who would have thought the old man to have had so much blood in him."

So much blood? The crime scene was drenched with liters of Steve York's blood. And Steve hadn't been an old man, easy to kill. He'd been young and strong, with so much living before him. Yet someone had taken a knife and stabbed him so grievously that he had bled until his heart had nothing left to beat.

Her phone rang again. "Carol Ashton." She raised her eyebrows. "Here? Yes, all right, I'll see her."

Madeline Shipley made an entrance into Carol's office, bestowing a brilliant smile upon the officer who had escorted her there. Madeline was accustomed to making entrances, Carol thought. And accustomed to the effect she had on people.

"I like your show," said the young man, red faced. He cast a look at Carol and began an awkward retreat.

Madeline stopped him with a hand on his arm. "Thank you. I appreciate that."

Carol gave a wry smile. Banal words, but delivered by a beautiful woman with gleaming copper hair, gray long-lashed eyes, a husky, confiding voice, and a highly-rated nightly news show on television, they had a telling potency. The officer, blushing even more, nodded and backed out the door.

Carol waited until the door closed, then said, "To what do I owe this pleasure, Madeline?"

She was surprised to see her here. Usually Madeline kept her personal life rigorously quarantined from her professional persona, a necessity for someone so firmly in the closet.

Madeline seated herself and smoothed the skirt of her supremely well-cut charcoal suit. "I'd rather hoped for a considerably warmer welcome, Carol," she said. "Especially since I haven't seen all that much of you lately." She gave Carol a wicked smile. "And you know how much of you I like to see."

"I'm on a case —"

"I know. Detective Sergeant York. His neighbors, Marge and Ed Parcell, will be on *The Shipley Report* tonight." Madeline grinned. "I suppose you met Marge Parcell?"

24

Carol lips twitched. Even under the circumstances of this morning's interviews, it would have been impossible not to respond to Parcell's wife, one way or the other. Carol had been expecting an aged little woman to match her husband. Instead, Marge had turned out to be fully twenty years younger than Parcell, a tall, thin woman with dyed red hair piled high on her head, bright inquisitive eyes, a loud raucous voice and a bellowing laugh.

"I did meet her. I'm sure she'll be a hit on your program," she said.

Carol leaned back and surveyed the beautiful woman on the other side of her desk. As always, she felt the stirring of physical attraction. Also as usual, she felt exasperated at Madeline's unfailing confidence that Carol in some way belonged to her.

"Madeline, you know I'm busy . . ."

"I've come to say good-bye."

Carol blinked. "Good-bye?"

"I've just managed to score an unexpected interview with the new powers-that-be in Hong Kong, followed by audiences with several high-ranking politicians in China, plus, would you believe, a commie pop band and a couple of film stars." She looked complacent. "The network is ecstatic and wants me to complete a tour of the whole of Southeast Asia to give a popularized snapshot of the region. The usual stuff — ordinary lives contrasted to what the leaders say. I'll be broadcasting live from a different country every day or so."

It was the sort of thing Madeline's program did so well. There would be a brief appearance by a selected politician, dignitary, star, or celebrity of the moment, followed by an in-depth exposé of "the real story." Or, as *The Shipley Report* promos always said, "The news behind the news."

Carol steepled her fingers. "It sounds very interesting."

Madeline chuckled at Carol's noncommittal tone. "No words of gloom at my pending absence?" Her smile faded and she leaned across the desk to put her hand over Carol's linked fingers. "I hope you'll miss me — a lot."

"Madeline, this isn't the time —"

"Or place? You're quite right, but I'm flying out this evening straight after the show, and I had to see you."

Her guard down, Madeline looked into Carol's eyes. "I do love you, Carol. You must know that." There was a long moment, then Madeline went on, "How's Sybil?"

Carol sighed. "Come on, Madeline . . ."

Back into her persona, Madeline smiled. "As if Sybil has a ghost of a chance with you," she said.

Carol heard Mark Bourke greet Madeline in the hall on her way out, then he came in to her office, shutting the door behind him. "They've found the van." His homely, pleasant face was drawn, and he looked exhausted to the point of sickness.

She pushed back her chair. "Where?"

"On a back road near Pitt Town. It'd been torched, but the signwriting on the side was still visible. That's how we got word so fast. I've got the local cops securing the area, and I've sent out a team to look at the site. They'll bring the van back to the crime lab on a truck."

"Too much to hope someone saw who dumped it?"

He nodded wearily. "Too much to hope."

He folded his long body onto one of Carol's uncomfortable straight-backed wooden chairs. "Anne says she's got a handle on the signwriter who did the van."

"Yes, we're seeing him this afternoon. How are you going on Steve's cases? Anything there?"

Revenge was always a possibility in a cop killing, and Steve had arrested or testified against his share of violent criminals.

"Nothing jumps out, Carol, but we've just looked at the current ones so far." Bourke ran a hand over his face. "Jesus," he said, "I feel like a truck's hit me."

Carol looked at him with sympathy. "How's Lauren?" she asked.

He gave a pained grunt. "What do you expect, Carol? Last time I looked, she wasn't dancing in the streets."

"I didn't imagine she would be."

He put up a palm in apology. "Sorry. This has really got to me."

"We have to interview her as soon as possible." When Bourke grimaced, she moderated her business-like tone to say more gently, "You and Pat knew them well as a couple. Is there any possibility that a past boyfriend of Lauren's was holding a grudge against Steve?"

He thought for a moment. "There was some guy

27

she was going with when she met Steve, but I don't think there was any real problem when he and Lauren broke up."

"Steve wasn't killed by a stray homicidal maniac who wandered in off the street. Someone went to a lot of trouble. Get the boyfriend's name from Lauren and follow it up, Mark."

"Pat's with Lauren . . ." He shook his head. "It's really rough, Carol, when this happens to someone you're close to."

"Do you want me to take you off the case?"

"No!" He straightened in the chair. "I want to be the one to nail the fucking bastard."

BRADLEY'S SIGNWRITING SERVICES the freshly painted door declared in impeccable lettering that matched the signwriting on the small van in the parking area. The rest of the small industrial mall was not so exemplary. There was a shabby, defeated air about most of the other businesses: a locksmith's neon had only half the name illuminated; an upholstery fabric wholesaler had a cardboard sign tacked to the door indicating an unexplained closure of several days; someone had scrawled over OFFICE EQUIPMENT SELLOUT the laconic words, *Gone Bust*.

When Carol opened the door to Bradley's Signwriting Services, a bell jangled, and almost simultaneously a diminutive ginger-haired young man wearing spotless white overalls and wiping his hands on a rag, appeared.

Standing behind the little counter, he looked from

Carol to Anne Newsome, then back again. "You're Inspector Ashton," he said. "I liked what you did with that militia group. Took real guts."

Carol gave a brief nod to acknowledge his praise. Her public profile, always high, had been pushed up a few notches more by the media attention she'd received during her last big murder case.

"This is Constable Newsome," she said. "You spoke to her on the phone about some signwriting you did on a van."

Bradley opened a leaf in the counter and indicated they should come through. "I've pulled the paperwork," he said. "Come through to the office."

Carol took one of his business cards displayed in a Perspex stand on the counter, then followed Anne into the office. This was a grand name for a cramped little room almost entirely filled by a black metal desk with a swivel chair squashed behind it, a black three-drawer filing cabinet, and two mismatched wooden chairs painted with black enamel. She could see through to a short hall that led to the back door, beside which was a tiny sink filled with tins and brushes.

He positioned the two chairs for them, then squeezed behind his desk and sat down. Carol was not surprised to find that the surface of the desk was a great deal tidier than her own. The black plastic in-tray had only a moderate stack of papers: the out-tray held only a couple of stamped envelopes for mailing.

She glanced at the business card and raised her eyebrows fractionally. He had been watching her. "Yes, it's true," he said with a grin. "My name's Brad

Bradley. It's actually Bradley Bradley, but I couldn't come at that. At least it's good for business, because no one forgets my name."

She returned his smile. "I can see why it's easy to remember."

"This is my own company," he said with pride. "Only been running a year, and I'm already in the black." He slanted his head reflectively. "Of course, Dad helped me with a loan to set it up, so it isn't really all my own work."

Although she was impatient to get down to work, Carol let Anne respond with relaxed small talk, taking the opportunity to assess the young signwriter. She was already favorably impressed by his manner and the way that he kept his business place. He was in his early twenties. Well below average height, he had a round, pleasant face, and his general impression of meticulous order was only spoiled by the irrepressible spring of his ginger hair.

Carol was about to bring the conversation back to the reason for the interview when Bradley said, "But you'll be wanting to ask me about the Terror of Insects guy. It's to do with the murder of the cop, isn't it?"

Anne opened her notebook. Carol said, "Yes, it is. Anything you can tell us would be helpful."

"Okay." Bradley gazed at the ceiling, marshaling his thoughts. "The guy called me on a Monday, just two weeks ago today. Said his name was Brian July. I remember I said something about that, and he said July was some old English name. He told me he'd got my name out of the phone book. I usually go to wherever the client is, even if I'm doing a vehicle, but he insisted on coming here that afternoon."

Carol felt exultation rise in her throat. Bradley was the kind of witness who would remember details about another person. "So you got a good look at him."

"Sure did."

"I'll ask you for a detailed description later, but what were your first impressions?"

"He was in his thirties, I thought. He was thin — looked fit. Taller than me." He grinned. "Like, almost everyone's taller than me. He was around average height, I'd say, or maybe a centimeter or two more. Brown hair, glasses. No one you'd particularly notice in the street."

Now Carol could form a mental picture of her quarry, but she knew it was likely that at least the hair and glasses would be easily changed.

"Go on about what happened."

"He turned up on time, around two o'clock, and sat exactly where you're sitting, Inspector. He told me he was starting his own business as an exterminator, and we had a bit of a talk about that for a while. I said how hard it was to get a customer base, and he said that he was going to pick a different area every few weeks and drop leaflets in the mailboxes offering free inspections for termites as a come-on."

"Did he mention any particular areas where he intended to do this?"

"Not that I remember. I said there was an awful lot of competition in the field — big players — and he laughed and said he had a surefire name for his company that would get attention. When he told me it was *Terror of Insects* I thought it was pretty stupid, but I kept that to myself."

Bradley pointed toward his black in-tray. "The

signwriting quote I gave him is there on the top of the pile, if you want to see it."

Carol stood up to look at the quotation, but she didn't move it. "Brian July didn't give you an address or telephone number."

"It didn't seem necessary. I was doing the work here, and he was going to pay me in cash."

"This is the original?"

"Yeah, he didn't take it with him. Stupid that, because it was a business expense, and he'd need it for taxes."

"But he touched the paper?" When Bradley frowned at her, she added, "I'm thinking of fingerprints."

He pressed his fingers against his lips while he thought. "Jeez, that's funny," he said at last, "I don't think he did. We talked about exactly what he wanted, we went outside and I looked at the van — it was white, secondhand, but in very good condition — then we came back in here and I wrote out the quote."

"You didn't hand the paper to him at any stage?" Carol felt both exasperated and resigned. For a moment she had hoped, but already she was sure she was dealing with someone who wouldn't make it easy to obtain identifying fingerprints.

"No, the guy sort of twisted his head around and read it while it was in front of me, and he said it was a fair price and he'd be paying cash. I couldn't do the work for him until the next morning because I had a job that afternoon, but he said that was okay."

Bradley went on to explain how Brian July had turned up the next morning at eight and how he had completed the signwriting and been paid in cash. "He was pleased with my work. Gave me a bonus on top of the figure I'd quoted him. Didn't want a receipt — just drove off."

"We want to fingerprint this office, in case he touched a surface."

Bradley seemed to understand for the first time that he had been in the company of a probable murderer. "Hell," he said. "He was a nice guy. Are you sure he . . .?"

"At the moment he's just a possible witness. We would like to question him about some matters." Carol's soothing words didn't calm the alarm that was filling Bradley's face.

"Jeez!" he said. "Do you think he could come back here?"

"It's not likely," said Carol, not putting into words the thought, *If he really believed you could identify him, he would have been back to get you before now.*

CHAPTER FOUR

The sunroom of Lauren's parents' place was crowded with ferns and cactus plants in a variety of brilliantly colored plastic and pottery containers. There was a pervasive smell of damp earth, and, although the ferns seemed luxuriant and healthy, most of the cacti looked sick or dying.

Overwatering, thought Carol, irritated. She knew it was absurd, but the mistreatment of plants really annoyed her. For a moment she was amused with herself. Maybe she had been imbued with some of her Aunt Sarah's reverence for life.

Reverence for life? The weight of the sights, sounds and smells of the postmortem she had attended that morning swept over her. Washed clean, Steve's body had shown the full extent of the butchery: his neck slit so that blood from his carotid artery had gushed into his windpipe; slashing stab wounds to his chest and stomach; deep puncture wounds in his back.

Apart from superficial cuts to Steve's hands and face, Jeff Duke had detailed eleven serious injuries, all inflicted by a large, double-bladed knife. Any of five of these could have caused death within minutes.

"I know you've heard this before," Jeff Duke had said, pausing with his gloves red with Steve's blood, "but it's true to say he never had a chance. It was a frenzied attack so sudden that he hardly had time to react."

Carol willed away the picture of Steve's body lying filleted, the abdominal cavity awash with clotted blood, the lungs darkly saturated. With an effort, she concentrated on the sunroom.

It was not a comfortable place. There were four stiff plastic chairs with flat floral cushions, and a long yellow vinyl settee of unparalleled ugliness. Carol was perched on one of the chairs, Mark Bourke, a leather folder beside him, sat beside Lauren on the settee. His expression was somber, and he'd nicked his chin when shaving.

Lauren's eyes were red, and she clutched a balled-up handkerchief in one hand, but, at least for the moment, the weeping was over. Usually fastidious, she seemed oblivious of her appearance, wearing a faded blue dress, and her feet were bare. Haggard, her hands trembling, she seemed to have aged years from the giggling young woman Carol had last seen.

She was slightly built, with long brown hair and a pointed, pixie face. Privately, Carol had considered her facile and shallow, but any previous thought of Lauren's unworthiness for Steve was submerged by shared grief and the sympathy Carol felt for anyone who had suffered such a tragedy.

"Lauren, I'm so sorry we have to ask you these questions, but I'm sure Mark's explained to you why it's so important."

Bourke shifted uneasily at his name, and the yellow vinyl squeaked under his weight. Carol had tried to persuade him to let Anne Newsome take his place, but he had vehemently insisted on being present for the interview.

"I understand." Her voice was hoarse, so unlike her usual light soprano that Carol was startled. "Anything I can do . . . Anything."

"Mark's already spoken to your last boyfriend, Stu Hope, and it seems you parted on good terms. Is that true?"

"Stu? You can't think he'd have anything to do with this. He's got another girlfriend. They're engaged. He wouldn't care what I did."

"And there's no one else you've had a relationship with that could bear a grudge because you and Steve were together?" Carol chose her words carefully. She wanted to avoid the word marriage — the loss was too raw to remind Lauren of what lay ahead . . . a funeral instead of a wedding.

"No one. Who could..." Lauren's voice trailed off and she began to rub her forehead, her long pink fingernails scoring grooves in the skin.

Carol wanted to reach out and stop the action, but instead she said, "Did you know that Steve had been talking to an exterminator about having an inspection of the house?"

Lauren dropped her hand. She looked at Carol vaguely, then said, "Yes, I remember. Steve was really pleased because the guy said he could have a free inspection for white ants, so there was no cost unless he found something. We've been saving money. It sounded like a good deal."

"You didn't meet this exterminator?"

"No. Steve said he came to the door one Saturday. Said he was drumming up business in the area and that he would undercut anyone else who quoted for pests. White ants, cockroaches — everything."

"Did you hear his name?" Carol said.

"Something funny...a month. June? No, July, I think."

Bourke cleared his throat. "Can you tell us anything else about this man?"

She shook her head. "No. Steve said he had called his business something that was just too cute to be true, but I don't remember what it was."

Carol nodded to Bourke, who slid a sheet out of his leather folder. Handing it to Lauren, he said, "This is the police artist's likeness of the man who had the sign done on the van the exterminator used. Look at it carefully and see if it reminds you of anyone you know, or have seen in the past."

Carol had sat in on Bradley's session with the artist and had been impressed by the young signwriter's attention to detail as he answered the questions and was guided to use the identikit components to build a likeness. She had confidence that they would end up with a good impression of what the suspect had looked like then. What he looked like *now* was another matter.

The page fluttered in Lauren's fingers. She tried to hold it steady with both hands as she studied the image. "Is this the man that . . ." She pressed her lips together. Tears filled her eyes.

Bourke put a hand on her shoulder. "Lauren, we don't know. It's a possibility. Have you ever seen him before?"

She dabbed at her eyes with her handkerchief, then stared at the illustration again. Carol knew exactly what she was seeing — a thin face, undistinguished in its blandness, with straight medium-length hair parted on the right side. Whoever he was, he looked relentlessly average in height, build and features.

Lauren sighed. "I don't know him." She turned to Bourke. "Why would he do it? Why?"

"We don't know yet." He gently took the sheet from her and returned it to the folder.

Carol changed the subject. "Lauren, has anything unusual happened lately?"

Her frown was fretful. "Unusual? What do you mean?"

"Did Steve mention anything to you that he thought was strange? Something like a phone call, or meeting someone unexpectedly. Anything out of the ordinary."

"There was that letter."

Bourke shook his head gently when Carol looked

at him. This was obviously the first he had heard of any letter.

"Tell me about it," said Carol.

She shrugged. "It was some dumb chain letter. Steve got it in the mail last week. He showed it to me, but I didn't bother reading it."

"Do you remember anything about it?"

"There was a quote at the top. 'For they have sown the wind, and they shall reap the whirlwind.' " The faintest smile appeared on Lauren's lips. "Surprised I know a quote from the Bible? I taught Sunday school for years."

"How did Steve react?"

Lauren locked her hands together until the fingers were white. "I never thought of it again, until now. I remember Steve saying it was the weirdest chain letter he'd ever seen."

She looked down at her hands, examining them as though they didn't belong to her. "He made a joke about what the letter said — if you broke the chain, you were going to die."

Carol had two books of quotations on her desk. Her battered old copy of Bartlett's *Familiar Quotations* merely noted the quotation Lauren had given as coming from Hosea, chapter eight, verse seven of the Bible. A more modern, and far less comprehensive, dictionary of quotations had placed *They have sown the wind, and they shall reap the whirlwind* under the general heading of "Consequences."

She began to doodle on a message pad. Supposing

for a moment that the chain letter was linked to the murder, what significance did a verse from the Bible have? She drew a square, heavily hatched, with an arrow leading to another square. Act and consequence. What had Steve done that somebody believed was so evil, that the outcome had to be a bloody execution?

She looked up at a knock on the door.

"Carol!"

"Kemp!"

They both smiled. It was an absurd ritual that had somehow developed over the years since she had first met Kemp Gray during the Internal Affairs briefing over the Moreno case. She had been investigating the murder of a police officer allegedly involved in drug payoffs, and Internal Affairs had released their files to her.

At the time she had been wary of Gray, having heard much about his reputation as a cynical, seen-it-all officer who was ruthless and uncompromising, but they had struck an immediate rapport.

Police Internal Affairs officers were usually looked upon with suspicion, sometimes loathing, by the ordinary cop. This had been especially true of late, when both the Independent Commission Against Corruption and the Wood Royal Commission had revealed serious problems of misconduct in some areas of the New South Wales Police Service. Police Internal Affairs had been involved in following up many of the specific allegations.

"Is this a social visit?"

Gray shut her office door firmly behind him. "No, Carol, it isn't."

Her mind skittered over a mental list of officers

40

in her department. Who in the hell was Internal Affairs after now? She could think of a few possible candidates . . . cops who skated close to illegalities in their dealings with criminal elements, but nothing that would bring the interest of someone as powerful as Kemp Gray.

"Sit down, Kemp. Coffee?"

"No thank you. I made the mistake of drinking that black glue you call coffee last time I was here."

He placed his black leather briefcase precisely on the floor beside the chair, then carefully unbuttoned his double-breasted suit coat before taking his seat. He had a bulldog face and bristling, prematurely white hair. Pear-shaped, heavy-thighed, with a splay-footed walk, Kemp Gray nevertheless did everything he could to disguise these disadvantages. He was always impeccably dressed, wearing hand-tailored dark suits, crisp white shirts, and a red or maroon tie. His meaty hands were manicured, and he wore a wide wedding ring on his left hand.

Carol was one of the few police officers who had met Kemp's wife, an alert, amusing woman confined by multiple sclerosis to a wheel chair.

"How's Marion?"

Gray's ugly-attractive face softened. "Not bad, Carol. Not bad at all. Her sight's not good at the moment, but they say there might be a new treatment . . ."

Carol knew that he had spent a small fortune chasing a cure or searching for anything that might help alleviate the symptoms of his wife's disease. "Give her my love," she said.

"You must come and see us. It's been ages."

Carol smiled. "After this case, I promise."

"This case. Yes." The usual forbidding expression was back. "It's about Sergeant York. That's why I'm here."

Frankly astonished, Carol said, "You're not going to tell me Steve York has got a file in Internal Affairs?"

"More than one. As a matter of fact, he figured in two past investigations, but nothing came of them. When I heard he'd been killed, I pulled the files. There's a slim possibility there's some connection to his murder."

Leaning over to open his briefcase, he said, "Did you ever run across an Inspector Samuel Orbe?"

Carol had an instant mental picture of a tall, rangy man who had always been, unpleasantly, one-of-the-boys in the most sexist way. "I knew him, distantly. He took early retirement some time ago, didn't he?"

"Just one step ahead of the posse, Carol. Internal Affairs pretty well had him, but" — his lip curled — "*political* considerations surfaced. Orbe was allowed to retire gracefully, ostensibly for health reasons, on a full pension."

"I gather Orbe knew too much about certain people."

"You've got that right. The word came down from the top of government to let sleeping dogs lie."

"What's this got to do with Steve York?"

Handing her a manila folder, he said, "This is the guts of a file concerning the death of Constable Sako. You might remember, he was beaten to death during a melee outside an inner-city pub a few years back. Orbe was on the case, and assisting him was a constable by the name of York. They both gave evidence at the trial of the ringleader of the mob, one Gordo Costello."

Carol opened the folder. "They verballed Costello?"

Gray gave her a cynical smile. "Verballed, colluded on evidence, told lies under oath. There's no doubt the accused was as guilty as hell, there were enough witnesses to the attack, but nevertheless, he was really loaded up by the cops to make sure of a conviction."

Of course Carol was well aware of all the illegal methods certain officers used to build a water-tight case against a suspect. Historically, in some notorious police stations it had been almost an established mode of operation. The Wood Royal Commission had exposed the most egregious of the methods in use.

Verbals — also called *verballing* — involved the submission as evidence of unsigned records of interview and notebook confessions. In essence, the court was told that the accused had admitted to the police his or her guilt, but had then refused to sign a formal confession.

Visuals occurred when an arresting officer wrote a statement which was then sent by computer to colleagues, who each signed the copy as if it were their own statement, thus falsely corroborating the "evidence," including fictitious police notebook entries.

Scrumdowns involved officers conferring to refresh their memories of the modified, or completely fabricated, stories that would later be presented as hard facts to the court.

"Kemp, I can't see Steve York involved in falsifying evidence."

He raised a cynical eyebrow. "Surely you're not that naive, Carol. Remember when you were a wet-behind-the-ears constable? Those older and wiser than you said something was so — and it *was* so."

Reluctantly, she had to admit there was some validity in what he said. "Okay, I know that if a superior officer says something is true, it's hard to contradict if you're new at the job, but we're not talking a shading of facts here. This is straight-out corruption."

Gray pulled at the knee of his impeccable trousers, and crossed his legs. "To be charitable, I'd say it was simply that York wanted to get ahead, and when Orbe pushed him to bend the rules, he gave in. In fact, after Orbe retired, there was never another hint that York was misrepresenting evidence."

"So when Steve died, he was clean?"

"For some years. But people have long memories, Carol." He took a second folder from his briefcase and put it in front of her. "This is the second instance where Internal Affairs had a strong case against Orbe, and, by association, his assisting officer, Stephen York."

She opened the file. "The Reginald Ular trial. This is what . . . six or seven years ago?"

"Seven years, last July. I have a reason to know, because Sam Orbe certainly made false statements under oath, and the evidence he gave was corroborated by Constable Stephen York."

Reginald Ular had been tried for the murder of twelve-year-old Sally Ingersoll, found guilty, and given a life sentence.

"I remember there was a campaign to set aside the verdict and have a new trial," Carol said. "I presume Internal Affairs records would have been subpoenaed to prove police misconduct."

"Indeed, that would have happened; however, last year Reginald Ular died in a prison riot at Bathurst Jail." He spread his hands. "Case closed."

Kemp Gray's expression told Carol there was something more. "Okay, Kemp, what is it?"

"Perhaps it's a coincidence, but Sam Orbe was killed late last year in a car accident. He was run off the road near Wyong, slammed into a tree, and died instantly. A witness saw the truck that sideswiped him, but the driver floored it and disappeared. Never found the truck. Never found the driver."

"What are you saying? That the same person killed Orbe, and then Steve?"

"I'm not saying anything, except that it's an interesting conjunction of facts, Carol."

"Did Sam Orbe die before or after Reginald Ular?"

A smile creased his heavy cheeks. "Good question. After. Ular was killed in prison in November last year. Orbe had his car crash in mid-December."

"A crash that could have simply been an accident."

"True, Carol, but it happened on a straight stretch of road where there was no safety fence. Orbe's car was sideswiped by an nondescript truck with interstate plates, that then completely disappeared. Call me over-suspicious, but I wonder if there isn't a link with York's death."

"I suppose I'd better look at the accident report."

"No sooner said" — Kemp Gray reached into his briefcase — "than done." He handed Carol several stapled pages. "I took the liberty of getting a copy for you."

Carol sat back and regarded him. "You really

think there's something in this, don't you?" She
frowned, struck by a sudden thought. "Reginald Ular
was a pedophile . . ."

Gray gave the muffled snort that was his trade-
mark laugh. "You're thinking of Operation Speedo?"

This was the name of a Internal Affairs operation
that had investigated the links between a so-called
pedophile brotherhood and the corrupt police bribed
to protect them from prosecution.

"I was thinking that maybe Orbe was paid to
somehow fix the court case, and he fell down on the
job."

Gray's jowls wobbled as he shook his head. "You
can say a lot a bad things about Inspector Samuel
Orbe, but that isn't one of them. In fact, he was dis-
ciplined several times early in his career for roughing
up suspected pedophiles. He hated them. I'm sure
that's one of the reasons he perjured himself in the
Ular case — he wanted to put the man away for
good."

"If you're right — and I'm not saying for one
moment that you are — then I'm looking for someone
who wants revenge for Reginald Ular's death."

Gray stood up and buttoned his coat. "Let me
know when you find him, Carol," he said.

CHAPTER FIVE

Carol was leaning back in her chair reading through the report on the accident that had killed Orbe when Bourke stuck his head around the door. "Had a visit from Kemp Gray, I hear. Which one of us is for the high jump?"

He was only half joking. The various royal commissions had been assiduous in the search for corruption, and many long-term police officers had somewhat questionable incidents in the past, when the law enforcement ethos had been rather more lax regarding scrupulous attention to the rules of evidence.

She passed him the pages she'd been reading. "Remember Inspector Samuel Orbe? He died in a car crash last year. Kemp thinks there could be a tie-in with Steve's murder."

Suddenly alert, Bourke sat down while she filled him in with the details. He rubbed his jaw reflectively when she finished. "Looks like a very long shot to me, particularly if Orbe was in the habit of loading up crims. That would give us any number of people who'd love to see *him* dead — but Steve is only supposed to have a connection with two cases.' He narrowed his eyes. "And I don't believe it, anyway."

"There were two that Internal Affairs investigated," said Carol, "but Steve could have been involved in others."

Bourke stared at her. "This is Steve we're talking about." He was flushed, and Carol realized with surprise that he was furious with her. "We aren't talking about some run-of-the-mill crooked cop."

Knowing that neither of them had had enough sleep and that the stress of investigating the slaughter of someone they both knew well was adding to the tension, she said mildly, "Steve doesn't have to be guilty of tampering with evidence — someone just has to believe that he has. Just keep it in mind as a possible motive."

He nodded slowly. "Okay, I'll do that." His conciliatory tone was a concession that he knew that his response had been unreasonable.

"Anything on the exterminator's van?"

"Not yet. The interior was doused with petrol and

set on fire. No weapon, no fingerprints, or anything else worthwhile, although there is something that looks like melted plastic in one corner. They'll get back to us on that. The license plates were stolen from a van in a secondhand dealer's yard three weeks ago. We're circulating the engine number to all states."

Finding herself drumming her gold pen against the side of her overflowing in-tray, Carol put it down and made a conscious effort to relax. "Liz Carey called me. She's pretty well drawn a blank, too. Her team went over the whole house, inside and out, and basically found nothing. Of course there are some unidentified prints, but no one with a record. And there's no sign of a chain letter or envelope."

Carol had decided not to release the information that the victim had received a threatening chain letter prior to his death. She wasn't convinced that it was anything but a coincidence that he got it the week before he died, but if there was a connection, withholding this specific could be a key factor in the future interrogation of a suspect.

Bourke grunted. "The letter's a red herring." He got up and began to pace around the office. "The loonies will start calling soon, now that the identikit's gone to the media and Ferguson's showing the picture door-to-door in Steve's neighborhood." He rammed his fists into his pockets and glared out the window at the wall opposite. "Probably a waste of time. Whoever he is, he's smart, so he'll have changed his appearance by now."

There would be plenty of calls, Carol knew that, and chasing them down would be frustrating and time consuming. People would be convinced that the description fitted the man reading the gas meter, the refrigerator repairman, the old guy who fed pigeons in the park, the next-door neighbor's layabout son. But every tip had to be checked out — it only needed one to hit gold and lead to the suspect.

Bourke still stood with his back to her, and the tension in his shoulders was obvious. Absently, she noted with affection that, although he had his hair cropped short in an effort to disguise his advancing baldness, he was fighting a losing battle. He was always so dependable, sure and tenacious, that it was somehow touching to her to see him defeated, even in such a small way.

She said, "Did you turn up any serious conflicts in Steve's family or with his friends?"

"There were a few disagreements and fights, but that comes to all of us, just with living." He swung around to her. "Carol, this murder is revenge for some terrible, imagined wrong, not a family squabble. And it's someone willing to wait, to plan it down to the last detail. He spent time getting a van, having a name put on it, and creating a role for himself."

"Someone with a sense of humor."

"What?"

"The name, *Terror of Insects*. It's whimsical."

"I'm not laughing."

Anne Newsome was on the phone. Her battered desk was covered with papers and files. A half-full mug of coffee was at her elbow, a doughnut with one bite out of it nestled on a paper bag beside it.

50

"Thank you," Anne was saying, "we do appreciate your help, Mr. Evans."

Replacing the receiver, she rolled her eyes at Carol. "Mad as a two-bob watch," she said. "Rings every time we have a murder. He always says it's his landlady. Doesn't matter if it's a man — it's his landlady in drag."

"Anne, I want everything you can get on a man called Reginald Ular. He was tried and convicted for the murder of a young girl about seven years ago." Before Anne could protest, Carol added, "I know you've got a lot on your plate, but this could be important."

"Apart from the official reports, what do you want?"

Carol smiled, liking Anne's can-do attitude. "I know it's a pain, but will you get newspaper clippings, any available transcripts of the trial, photos — in short, anything that refers to Reginald Ular and people associated with him. He died last year in a jail riot, so it would help if you could turn up something on that too."

"You want it right away?"

"Drop everything else. I'd like it today."

It was late when Carol pulled into the street-level carport above her home. There was room for two cars, and she realized that she always parked as though Sybil was going to pull in beside her. Looking at the empty spot, she thought of Madeline's words, *As if Sybil has a ghost of a chance with you.*

Madeline had it wrong. It was the other way around. It was Sybil who had retreated to her house on one of the most beautiful of Sydney's northern beaches.

Suddenly, urgently, Carol had to know the measure of the situation.

She collected her bulging briefcase and walked down the front path. She could smell the spring flowers and the subtle eucalyptus scent of the bushland surrounding her house. She was greeted at the front door by Sinker and Jeffrey, their feline voices raised in serious protest. Carol felt a twinge of guilt, remembering that she'd forgotten to ask her ever-obliging neighbor to feed them tonight.

"Sorry fellows, I'll get you that food, quick smart."

Down the hall they wove intricate patterns in front of her, complaining all the way to the kitchen. Sybil's ginger Jeffrey was particularly outraged, making it clear that this dilatory performance from Carol was entirely unsatisfactory.

She opened two tins, both exactly the same fish dinner — experience had taught her that variety would be a cause of affronted pique — and carefully set them down the requisite distance apart on the wooden deck outside the kitchen. A sleepy bird chirped in the overhanging gumtrees, and with a rustle and thump, a mother possum with a wide-eyed baby clinging to her back landed on the railing. Carol knew the routine, handing her a peeled banana. The possum seized it in her claws, and balancing on her hind legs, with the baby looking over her shoulder, she began to take delicate mouthfuls.

The cats, intent on dinner, ignored any other activity. Carol's Sinker, sleekly black and white, eyed

Jeffrey sideways as they both ate. Carol smiled indulgently at him. He was quite capable of swiping anything he could get, should Jeffrey's attention wander.

Resolved, she went inside, picked up the phone, and punched in Sybil's number. "It's Carol. Sorry to ring so late, but I wonder if I could call by tomorrow? About ten? Okay, I'll see you then."

She wasn't hungry, but she found a frozen spaghetti dinner and dumped it in the microwave. She poured herself a straight Scotch and sat down on a kitchen stool to look through the material on Reginald Ular that Anne had managed to collect.

The case had received extensive coverage at the time. Reginald Ular was depicted as a charming, volatile personality who had been a shrewd businessman, making his money in X-rated videos sold legally by mail order from companies registered in the Australian Capital Territory. He was also a pedophile, and supplied hard-core child pornography to a wide clientele under the guise of sports and music videos.

The microwave gave a series of insistent beeps. Carol took another gulp of Scotch, then dumped the spaghetti dinner onto a plate. It looked rather like a mass of writhing worms, topped by a reddish brown viscous liquid. She stirred it to distribute the sauce and, fork in hand, went back to the material on Ular.

Chewing absently, she flipped through newspaper clippings of his arrest. Ular had persuaded his next-door neighbor, a single mother who had a drinking problem, to let him take "artistic photographs" of her twelve-year-old daughter, Sally. He provided generous payments to the mother for what he called "professional services." During each session he molested the young girl, terrifying her into silence with threats that he would kill both her and her mother if she said anything about it.

Carol's mouth twisted in revulsion. She pushed away the half-eaten spaghetti, poured herself another shot of Scotch, and continued reading.

There was debate about what happened next. Reginald Ular claimed that Sally Ingersoll had been accidentally asphyxiated during consensual bondage sex: the police declared that, enraged when Sally told him she had confided what was happening to a teacher, Ular had deliberately strangled her, then tried to dispose of the body. He was charged with sexual assault and murder.

The trial was notable for the ugly details of Ular's activities and the sobbing declarations of the mother that she had no idea what was happening when her daughter went next door for her photographic sessions.

Found guilty of Sally Ingersoll's murder, Reginald Ular made a statement to the court where he repeated his defense — that Sally had enthusiastically entered into their sexual activities together and that her death had been a dreadful accident that had broken his heart.

Although impassioned crowds outside the court screamed for his lynching, Ular was sentenced to the maximum under the law, life imprisonment with no possibility of release.

Carol studied a newspaper photograph of the man. He had a clear, open face and a broad, generous mouth. She knew, all too well, that a child molester rarely matched the popular stereotype of a shifty-eyed, loose-lipped deviate. It was cheerful Uncle Charlie, or the guy who coached sports teams in his own time, or, in the greatest betrayal of all, a child's own father.

She also knew, although it was no excuse, that it was extremely likely that, as a child, Reginald Ular had been molested himself, probably repeatedly.

Carol rubbed her eyes, and sighed. She couldn't read any more of this tonight. She'd get up very early, go for a run, and finish it before she saw Sybil.

Sybil. She felt both pleasure and apprehension. Pleasure that she would be seeing her in a few hours, apprehension of what that meeting might bring.

CHAPTER SIX

Just before dawn Carol was up and putting on her running shoes. The injury she had sustained to her face, and then the plastic surgery, had disrupted her early morning exercise routine, and she was still trying to get back to her former level of fitness.

Under her loose T-shirt she strapped on a belt holster. Checking the wicked little palm-size Glock 27 subcompact took a moment, then she shoved it into the holster positioned in the small of her back. It had saved her life before, and since that desperate time she had carried it, even when running very early in the deserted Seaforth streets or in the bushland reserve that bordered Middle Harbour.

She hurried through her stretching routine — she'd read somewhere that it made no difference whether you warmed up before running or set off straightaway, but she wasn't willing to run the risk of pulling a muscle and throwing out her exercise routine even further.

Olga was waiting at the side gate of her neighbor's place. The German shepherd gave several excited yips when she saw Carol. "Quiet, girl," whispered Carol as she opened the gate and let her out. Olga had been Carol's running companion for years and obviously keenly missed her early morning gambol when Carol wasn't available.

They set off at a moderate pace, and soon Carol had attained an easy rhythm. The slap of her running shoes, first on concrete pavement, then on the dirt paths that wound through the bush, soothed her soul. Olga bounded along beside her, vibrant with enthusiasm. Led by fascinating smells or provocative rustles, she periodically made noisy side trips into the vegetation. This amused Carol, who believed that Olga had the fantasy that she would emerge with some prey in her jaws. This had never occurred, although now and then tardy possums were forced to make undignified scrambles up the closest tree while Olga stood on her back legs, front paws on the bark, staring longingly after them.

Carol tried to keep her mind clear, unfocused, so she could just let the scents and sounds of the morning fill her consciousness. Her breathing was like a metronome that timed her paces. The gorgeous liquid notes of magpies caroling floated through the trees. She smiled up at the branches overhead. It seemed to her that birds were at their busiest in the early morning. They had the sun to greet, breakfast to locate, and the day to plan.

Olga, who had been left behind while she investigated something tantalizing, came barreling down the narrow bush path and squeezed past Carol at full run, her pink tongue flapping out the side of her mouth. Forced to break stride, Carol slowed, and immediately all the thoughts that had been under control burst into her mind.

Fragmentary images jostled for attention: Steve's dead face; Lauren, usually so particular about her appearance, bedraggled by grief; the signwriter's neat office; Madeline's confident smile . . . And Sybil.

She would see Sybil this morning. A longing for stability, for acceptance, for affection untrammeled by power games, filled her. Hadn't she had that once with Sybil?

The question puzzled and frustrated her. Looking through the prism of emotion and memory, Sybil seemed to have a very different picture of the past than the one Carol saw. This morning she would find out if those opposing perceptions could be reconciled.

Carol walked up the drive to Sybil's house, turning at the top to look back at the waves rolling to break in creamy foam on the beige sand of the beach. It seemed so long ago — another lifetime — when she had stood on this spot for the first time.

She went up the stairs, hesitating before she rang

the bell. Sybil opened the door and smiled a polite welcome. "Hi. The coffee's almost ready."

She was wearing a green shirt to complement her red hair, and white jeans. Carol suddenly felt over-dressed in her cobalt blue suit. She really shouldn't be there, taking time off the case, but it had been a compulsion to do something in person. Not to let things drift any further.

"You look great," she said.

"So do you, Carol."

"Even my nose?"

Sybil inspected Carol's face dispassionately, as a friend might. "It does give you a certain haughty air, but didn't the plastic surgeon say it was just a matter of time, and it'd be good as new?"

"That's what he said." Carol made herself smile. "Not that I trust doctors very much."

She thought, *We were lovers, don't you remember? You were everything to me, and I thought I was to you.*

Once Sybil Quade had been merely another pos-sible suspect in a murder case. Carol recalled the tug of attraction she'd felt, the way Mark Bourke had joked about fiery redheads and their penchant for violent action.

As she followed Sybil into the sitting room, Carol said, "I was thinking about the first time we met."

"In Mrs. Farrell's office?" Sybil grinned at the memory. "I'll never forget that noxious green carpet. And you were so intimidating."

"Was I?"

"Don't be modest, Carol. You know that silken threat you project is part of your very effective

59

persona." There was only an easy amusement in her tone, but she still seemed distant, self-contained.

I've come here expecting — what?

Carol hated the uncertainty she was feeling. She felt a chill of unease. This meeting wasn't going to go the way she had hoped. Driving there, she had rehearsed it in her mind — what she would say, how Sybil would respond. There would be possibilities, opportunities. Now that scenario seemed hopelessly naive, stupidly optimistic.

"This is a lovely view," she heard herself say.

Framed by glass doors open to the warm morning air, the view was more than lovely, it was spectacular. The jagged profile of a sandstone headland plunged to a collar of tumbled rocks; the sky was a cloudless, vibrating blue, shading into the deeper tints of the ocean at the horizon. Seagulls wheeled, their harsh cries blending with the distant pounding of the breaking waves.

Nothing, surely, could go wrong on such a day. Suddenly she wanted to reawaken all that they had once had together.

"Sybil . . ."

Sybil let out her breath in a sigh. "Yes?"

"Between us. Can it ever be the same again?"

"No."

Carol was astonished at the despair she felt. "I can't believe that."

"You have to believe it. It's true."

Light and air flooded the room. Carol saw that the beauty had been leached away. Now all she saw was a pointless conjunction of land, sea, and sky.

She said, keeping her voice steady, "Do you

remember the first time we kissed? It was out there, on the front steps, in the dark."

She could almost feel Sybil's body against hers, the shock when their lips met . . .

"Of course I remember. And everything else." Sybil's lips quirked in a sardonic smile. "Inconvenient to remember everything, isn't it?"

"Madeline, you mean? Sybil, you'd left me, then."

Feeling an echo of the baffled rage that had filled her at that breakfast, more than a year ago, when Sybil had calmly announced that she was going to London and would be away at least twelve months, Carol demanded, "What was I supposed to do? Wait around on the off chance that you'd come back to me?"

"It isn't Madeline."

"What, then?"

"This isn't going to work, Carol."

"I love you. I've never stopped."

Sybil looked away first. "I'll get the coffee."

Seizing her arm, Carol said, "Don't you believe me?"

She nodded slowly. "I believe you. But it's always on your terms. It always has been, and it always will be."

"That isn't true."

"It's true for me."

Carol stared at her, silent.

"Carol, it's over. We've been apart for more than a year, and I learned, to my surprise, that I could live without you."

With the sickening conviction that whatever she said, whatever she did, Sybil had armored herself against any argument, Carol, putting every bit of self-mockery she could marshal into her voice, said, "I think this is my cue to say, can we still be friends?"

"I don't know." Sybil gave a faint smile. "We could try."

Carol's pager, clipped into the waistband of her skirt, vibrated against her. "Can I use the phone?"

When she put down the receiver, Sybil was watching her. "You have to go?"

"Yes."

As she got into her car, she looked back up at the house. Sybil was standing at the door, still watching her. Carol hesitated, then put up her hand in a gesture of farewell.

Driving away, she was saturated with a bleak grief that turned the bright day gray around her. *Maybe,* she thought sardonically, *It's just that I want what I can't have.*

From the northern beaches it took her over an hour in heavy traffic to get to her destination. The address she had been given was for a house on a small road running off Darling Street, the main thoroughfare of Balmain.

Balmain was one of her favorite suburbs, full of quaint terrace houses on narrow streets and always bustling with life. Bounded on three sides by Sydney Harbour, Balmain residents could enjoy contrasting views. In the near distance the towers of the city rose, and part of the massive gray arch of the Sydney Harbour Bridge could be seen from many houses. Closer to home, the wharfs and container terminals of the busy port facilities were full of activity at all times of day and night.

Carol had frequently browsed the weekend

markets, watched street performers, or visited one of the many pubs and restaurants. With a pang she recognized the popular Thai eatery on Darling Street where she and Sybil had often dined, jammed at a small table while a stream of delicious little helpings of contrasting flavors were delivered one after the other.

She found Orelia Street without difficulty. It was short, and had a dog-leg in the middle. Around this bend a row of narrow terraces crowded together protectively, ending in a tiny pub on the corner, whose patrons, beers in hand, had joined the throng of curious people blocking the road. There was a buzz of excitement galvanizing them, and they were disinclined to obey the red-faced local police officer who was attempting to shoo them out of way.

He looked up with a face dark with annoyance when he saw Carol's car slowly butting through the crush, and then, recognizing her, he gave an awkward salute and redoubled his efforts to clear the street.

Ignoring the NO PARKING AT ANY TIME, she stopped the car opposite number fourteen and sat still, absorbing the details of the street. Some of the gentrification that had transformed so many workers' cottages into up-market houses for upwardly-mobile people had come to Orelia Street, but not all of the row of terraces sported fresh paint and restored ironwork. Some still had the additions so hated by purists: a veranda filled in to make an additional room; others had taken down the spiked cast iron that guarded the front boundary and had installed brick or painted paling fences to provide privacy.

Number fourteen, however, although in need of a coat of paint, was in its original form. There was a

63

dark-green cast-iron fence with matching gate enclosing a tiny garden. The slender two-story building had a corresponding cast-iron railing running along the second floor veranda, which had French doors, tightly closed to the warm air.

Mark Bourke had obviously been waiting for her. He made his way across the street and opened the driver's door. "Female fatality. Name's Janet McGary. Looks like it was a pipe bomb."

Reinforced by officers from two patrol cars, inroads had been made in the swelling crowd. Carol stopped to say to an officer stringing crime-scene tape, "Warn them once, then arrest them if they cross the line."

Bourke grinned at her. "Wouldn't it be easier just to shoot them?"

Above there was a beat of blades, and a television helicopter chattered into view above the rooftops. Carol shook her head. "Isn't there anyone else that could do this? We've got our hands full, Mark."

"The super thought you'd be interested. There's some suggestion there was a chain letter involved."

She stopped short and looked at him. "You're kidding me."

"I'm not. Apparently the next-door neighbor heard the explosion around ten this morning, rushed in, and found the corpse. It was a pretty awful sight, and she was half hysterical, but after she'd dialed triple zero and got the emergency services on the way, she called her granddaughter, who just happens to be a constable at the local cop shop. Told her all about how Janet McGary had shown her a threatening chain letter that she was worried about. Like Steve's, it said she was going to die unless she copied the letter and passed it on. The granddaughter called Anne Newsome — they went through training together."

They walked through the front door, which led straight into a living room. There was the usual bustle of a crime scene. All the lights were on, as the heavily-curtained windows would keep the interior dim, even at midday. The furniture was heavy, dark wood, overpowering in the small space. There was a metal fireplace with a tapestry screen of an English thatched cottage with a garden of hollyhocks. Knickknacks crowded every surface.

Bourke nodded toward the stairs. "Up there. The body's already been removed."

The first flight went up to a tiny landing, then reversed direction to lead to a short hallway. Ned Cromwell met them at the door of the bedroom, which was at the back of the house. In the room behind him a photographer was taking photographs.

Every time Carol saw the bomb expert, she thought Ned Cromwell fulfilled the stereotype of a prissy accountant. His mousy hair was conservatively cut, his expression was earnest, his shoulders sloped sharply, so that the coat of his gray suit hung awkwardly on his skinny frame, and he spoke with precise, pedantic cadences.

He also had the aggravating habit of referring to colleagues as "people," and Carol wondered how far into the conversation he could go without referring to Mark and herself this way.

"Okay, Ned, what've you got?" she said.

"It was nothing complicated." He had a light voice, high for a man. "Just your standard pipe bomb." A shade of contempt passed over his face.

"Anyone could get details of how to construct one from hundreds of Internet sites. A bit of plastic tubing, black powder — or even match heads — and fuses . . ." He gestured with his attenuated fingers. "Easy to build."

He stood aside to let them into the room. "That's where it exploded, people." he said unnecessarily.

The crime-scene photographer, a bulky woman with a bad-tempered expression, gave them a curt nod, took a couple more shots, then lumbered out of the room.

Janet McGary's body had been removed, leaving a rumpled nest of sheets contaminated with blood and fragments of plastic and metal. The solid wooden headboard and the side of the nightstand had a matching abstract design of multicolored splatters — blood and brain tissue.

Ned Cromwell was looking a little more enthusiastic. "Very simple bomb," he said. "So it had no timer, like a clock, for instance. This sucker had a fuse that had to be lit."

He indicated the shredded pillow. "I took a good look at the body before they moved it. I'd say the bomb was lying on the pillow to the right of her head. Someone had to put it in position, and light the fuse."

"Which makes me wonder why she didn't wake up while all this was going on," said Bourke. "And what was she doing in bed? It was ten o'clock in the morning."

Cromwell shrugged. "That's your problem, people. I just stick to explosive devices." He looked at Carol. "Yes," he said, "I know. You want a full report as soon as possible."

She gave him full smile. "That'd be nice, Ned."

"I'll get to work, then."

Carol and Bourke went out into the hallway. "What do we know about Janet McGary?"

"Not much, yet. I got a couple of minutes with the neighbor, Mary Gavin, before her doctor arrived to give her a sedative. Apparently Janet McGary was a retired high school teacher, widowed five years ago, when her husband Louis died. After that, she lived a quiet life, very involved in her church — that sort of thing." He looked back into the room, where Cromwell was crouching down beside the bed picking something up with tweezers. "It's hard to imagine anyone wanting to hurt someone like that."

"How about children? Nothing like a nasty family feud to provide a motive."

"There're some photos in the living room." He led the way down the narrow stairs. "She's got a daughter, lives somewhere near Newcastle."

A black baby grand was jammed into a small room at the back of the house near the kitchen. Photos were arranged across the gleaming closed lid. "Janet McGary was a music teacher," Bourke said. He handed her a photograph in a gold frame. "Doesn't look like premeditated murder material, does she?"

The photo showed a couple squinting into the camera. Behind them pyramids rose into a cloudless sky. "Her husband?"

Bourke grinned at her. "Some detective you are! Turn it over, it's written on the back."

The writing was a spidery scrawl on the gray cardboard backing of the frame. *Lou and me, Egypt, 1988.*

Carol returned to the photograph. It seemed to have been blown up from a standard size, because the outlines were slightly fuzzy. Lou McGary was balding, round faced, with a wide, happy grin. Janet McGary's white hair was arranged in careful waves and, although she was smiling, her expression was a little wistful. She was slightly built, diminutive under the caressing arm her husband had draped across her shoulders.

"She looks like the generic little old music teacher," said Bourke. "I had one just like her at school. Threw me out of the choir because she said I was tone deaf."

He picked up another gold-framed photograph. "Here's the daughter."

The woman, a middled-aged and more solid version of her mother, was posing in robe and mortarboard, obviously at a degree ceremony. Carol checked the back. Written in the same tenuous hand was, *Alice. B.A. Dip.Ed.*

Carol put it back on the piano lid. "When can I see the neighbor who found her?"

Bourke shrugged. "Tomorrow at the earliest, I'd say. She was very upset, and the doctor made it clear he was going to give her something to knock her out so we cops couldn't pester her."

The phone in the kitchen rang. Bourke raised his eyebrows to Carol and moved to answer it. The fingerprint technician, who was packing up his equipment, nodded to him. "Go ahead, I've done it."

Bourke picked up the receiver. "Hello? Who is this, please?" He listened, then asked questions as he flipped open his notebook and wrestled with the cap of his pen.

He was on the phone a long time, and when he came back he looked intrigued. "That was the local Meals on Wheels. Apparently Janet McGary was due there this morning. She volunteered for a run twice a month delivering meals to old people in the area."

Carol's Aunt Sarah was also a Meals on Wheels volunteer in the Blue Mountains area, so Carol was familiar with the operation of deliveries. "It's normally done in pairs. One person drives while the other runs in and delivers the meals. Did Janet McGary have help?"

"That's what's so interesting, Carol. She did have a partner, a youngish man who is also a parishioner at the local Anglican church. But you know, he didn't turn up this morning, although he's always been very dependable before, and when they called, there was no answer."

He blew out his cheeks. "What do you bet he's just disappeared into thin air?"

CHAPTER SEVEN

While Carol stayed at Orelia Street to question any neighbors who knew Janet McGary, Bourke went to interview people at the local Meals on Wheels. They met two hours later outside the Anglican Church of St. Luke, a soot-stained but stately gray stone building with massive walls and stained-glass windows protected by heavy mesh. Overhead, a large square bell tower loomed.

"Don't get out," said Bourke, clambering into the passenger seat of Carol's car. He shoved a white paper bag at her. "Sandwiches. Got them at the local deli. I've eaten mine, and they're bloody good." He handed her a white paper cup with a plastic lid. "Coffee. Black, no sugar."

Until this moment, Carol hadn't thought of food, but suddenly she was ravenously hungry. She thanked him and bit with enthusiasm into the thick brown bread of a chicken and lettuce sandwich. "What happened at Meals on Wheels?" she asked around the mouthful.

"Not much. The people there are really pushed to get dinners out to every old person on their lists. Volunteers drop out all the time, and someone else has to take up the slack. They knew Janet McGary well, because she's been doing it for years, but as far as her delivery partner was concerned, anyone who even remembered him was vague. I've got the name he used, Jon Peterson, and a telephone number. No address. Anne's working on that, but it seems the number belongs to a dry cleaner in Rozelle, and he's never heard of anyone of that name."

Carol took a gulp of coffee, luxuriating in the taste and aroma. It might be served in a cardboard container, but it was nectar to her caffeine-starved body.

"When I left they hadn't found any trace of the chain letter the neighbor mentioned," she said.

She took another swallow of coffee and sighed with pleasure.

"Good, eh?" said Bourke, grinning.

"You've saved my life."

"Speaking of life," said Bourke, sobering, "I showed everyone the picture, hoping that someone would cry, That's him! I know his real name and address!" He turned down the corners of his mouth.

"Naturally, that didn't happen. The best I got was an uncertain agreement that it might be the guy who accompanied Janet McGary. No one was sure."

"He didn't use his own car to make the delivery runs?"

"No. Hers. Its missing, by the way. Old Holden, but in good condition. I've got an all points out for it."

The last mouthful of chicken sandwich and the final swallow of coffee were savored. Carol checked her gold watch. "His wife said Reverend Mette's only available until four-thirty, so we'd better go in."

The rectory of St Luke's was constructed of the same gray stone as the church, and it had a similar noble look of an aristocrat bravely experiencing difficult times. The minister's wife, a determined woman in denim overalls over a chartreuse T-shirt that declared *It's the Salvation, Stupid,* let them in. "I'm Nordica Anderson-Mette. Inspector Ashton, is it? And you'd be . . . ?"

Obedient to her questioning glare, he responded, "Sergeant Bourke."

"Right! I want you to know that Kenneth's working on his sermon, then he has an important meeting about the roofing slates." She pointed at a closed door. "His study." A final challenging stare, and she disappeared down a dingy corridor.

Carol gave Bourke a half smile. "Can't wait to see the minister."

She knocked, and a muffled voice told them to enter. The minister of St. Luke's Anglican church was nothing like his militant wife, being mild faced, with tightly curled graying hair, a deep cleft in his chin, and an expression of puzzled helpfulness.

His prominent Adam's apple bobbed above his stiff cleric's collar as he hurried to clear piles of papers and books from two seats. "Oh, so sorry! Forgot you were coming."

After he'd fussed around and got them settled, he gratefully retreated behind his cluttered desk to his shabby brown leather swivel chair, which creaked in protest at his weight.

Reverend Mette's study was pervaded by the faintly musty, bookish smell that Carol had always associated with prayer books and kneeling pads in ancient pews. The walls were lined with shelves, each crammed to overflowing with books, papers, folders, and a variety of odd items, including a broken piece of slate tiling, part of a pipe from a wind organ, a silver chalice that was green from lack of polishing, and a collection of small misshapen glass bottles in a variety of brown, violet, and green colors.

Seeing Carol looking at the bottles, Mette hastened to say, "Antiques. Dug them up when we were putting in the new ladies' lavatory for the parish hall. Date to last century, they tell me."

He rubbed his pale big-knuckled hands together. "Now, what can I do to help you . . ." He sneaked a look at the card Carol had handed him. "Ah . . . Inspector? You must pardon me, but I'm not altogether clear what it is you're here for."

"Is one of your parishioners a Janet McGary?"

"Indeed yes. Janet has been the mainstay of our choir for many years. Contralto. You can get plenty of people who want to sing soprano because it's the melody line, but good altos are very scarce. Her husband sang tenor before he died, although frankly, he would have been better off with the bass line, if you see what I mean."

"I'm very sorry to tell you that Ms. McGary died this morning," said Bourke.

His mouth fell open. "Died? Why didn't Nordica tell me?" He got to his feet, scrabbling ineffectually in the papers on his desk. "Where are my car keys?" Abandoning the search, he asked, "Was it an accident?"

Carol said, "There was an explosion in her house."

Mette sat down again, shaking his head. "I just spoke to Janet yesterday . . ." He shook his head again. "Was it a gas leak? Those old houses . . ."

"It seems to have been a bomb."

Carol's words obviously flabbergasted him. "A bomb? A *bomb*?"

"We're interested in her activities and anyone who may have seen her lately." Bourke's tone was bland.

Mette stared at him. "Seen her lately?"

Carol said briskly, "I believe Ms. McGary was involved in Meals on Wheels."

"Yes. Yes, for many years." Reverend Mette seemed grateful to have something mundane to discuss. "It's a fine service, you understand, for people who are shut-in, and who don't cook themselves a decent meal every day."

"Do you know who helped with her deliveries?"

"Indeed I do, Inspector. A new parishioner at St.

Luke's, Jon Peterson. A fine young man." He gave a self-deprecatory cough. "From my perspective I say young, but of course Jon would be in his thirties."

"Do you have an address for him?"

"Oh, I'm sure we do, if only for the delivery of our parish paper each month."

"Perhaps there might be a photo of Mr. Peterson at some church function?" Carol didn't have high hopes for this eventuality, and wasn't surprised when Reverend Mette shook his head.

"I'm afraid not, although he did want to become involved with our youth group ... It's too early for the summer picnic, you see, and we've had no fund-raising events in the last two or three months since he's joined our congregation."

Carol looked over at Bourke, and he responded by taking a sheet out of his folder and handing it to Reverend Mette. "Have you ever seen this man?" Bourke asked.

Mette glanced vaguely at the sheet, then his gaze sharpened. "Why, this could be Jon Peterson. The hair's different, and the cheeks are a little too full, but it could be him. I'll call Nordica. She'll know."

Summoned from the mysterious depths of the rectory, his wife gave the illustration a cursory glance. "Could be anybody," she snorted. She frowned suspiciously at Carol. "Isn't this the suspect for that policeman's murder? I saw it in the paper this morning."

"Nordica, dear, the officers are here about Janet McGary. It appears she was killed by a bomb, just a few hours ago. Terrible thing ... "

She didn't seem shocked by this information. "Janet McGary was it? Heard it on the radio news, out in the kitchen, but they didn't give a name."

"Such a loss."

His wife looked puzzled for a moment, then she gave a brief nod. "Oh, yes, of course. The choir. Could be a problem."

Bourke raised an eyebrow to Carol, then said to Nordica, "We would appreciate it if you could give the illustration a closer look."

Her husband peered over her shoulder. "Doesn't it resemble Jon Peterson? You know, that new, nice young man."

She pursed her lips. "I suppose so, at a push. But then, anybody might look like him — Peterson is a bit of a nonentity, isn't he?"

"Oh, I wouldn't say that. I wouldn't say that at all. Just because he's quiet —"

"Kenneth always sees the best in people," Nordica said to Carol, one woman to another. Her tone indicated that she considered this somewhat of a failing.

"I would have thought that was an occupational hazard," said Carol with a mild smile.

Nordica Anderson-Mette looked at her closely, then, apparently deciding that there was no hidden barb intended, handed back the drawing of the suspect, saying, "You'll be wanting to go on your way, then, since we can't help you further."

"We would like Jon Peterson' address," said Bourke.

This brought a derisive grunt from Nordica. "I'll get it for you from my computer file, but I don't imagine it will be much use. If he's a suspect in something serious, he'll be long gone by now."

A few moments later she was back. "I keep the database up to date, otherwise things around here would be a shambles." Casting a look at her husband, as if daring him to contradict her statement, she added, "No address. Seems Peterson never gave us one."

Her forbidding expression dissolved into an unexpected grin. "He's looking more suspicious by the moment, isn't he?" she said.

Driving back to headquarters in late afternoon traffic that clogged Victoria Road, Carol made a mental list of urgent items that needed attention.

Bourke was arranging for the Reverend Mette and the redoubtable Nordica to have a session with the police artist; the artist's amended rendition of the suspect, as well as the original identikit, had to be shown to parishioners; either she or Bourke had to attend Janet McGary's postmortem when it was scheduled; the neighbor, Mary Gavin, must be interviewed as soon as possible; Anne Newsome was to complete arrangements for a meeting with Janet McGary's daughter, who was on her way down to Sydney from Newcastle . . .

She felt tired, overwhelmed. Where was Steve York in all of this? Was there a link with the chain letters? Carol had made sure that nothing about the letter Steve had received had leaked to the media, so it couldn't be a case of someone deliberately copycatting.

The traffic ahead started, and when she was slow to move a driver cut in front of her. She blasted her horn in a furious tide of rage — then bit her lip. This was no time to be losing control. She needed to be cool, in command. The investigation of Steve York's death was complicated enough, but it seemed to be expanding to include the possibility of multiple murders, all linked in some way.

She'd told Mark Bourke that he had a lot of reading to do — everything about the Reginald Ular case, and the file on Inspector Orbe's fatal accident. If those two cases were connected to Steve's death, then what others waited to be discovered?

She groaned as the green light she'd been inching toward changed to amber, then red. At this rate she'd be stuck in traffic for ages, when she could be at her desk doing something constructive.

Her mobile phone chirped. She flipped it open impatiently. "Hello?"

Madeline's voice sounded clear and cheerful. "Hong Kong's not the same since the red hordes took it over."

Carol was too tired to grapple with Madeline's demands, her authoritative confidence that she knew what was best for Carol. Not wanting to talk at all, Carol forced some amusement into her voice as she said, "Be careful, Madeline. The line's probably tapped, and I don't imagine your political hosts would be overjoyed to hear a remark like that."

"Maybe, but I've got too much good stuff to be careful. You've just got no idea . . ." She launched into a highly defamatory story about an Australian politician's antics in China.

Allowing Madeline to talk — her caustic wit was usually highly entertaining — Carol stopped and started in traffic that was moving, she thought to herself, as rapidly as clotted blood.

Blood. Steve's blood. Janet McGary's blood.

"Carol? Are you there?"

"Yes, of course I am."

Madeline's voice faded, then came back again. ". . . Sybil, I wonder?"

"What? I didn't hear you, Madeline."

She laughed. "Or didn't want to hear me. I was asking if you'd seen Sybil since I left."

Carol drummed her fingers on the wheel. All the grief and anger from the morning at Sybil's house iced her voice. "Give it a rest, Madeline. I mean it."

Madeline's sigh gusted down the line. "Don't put yourself through it, darling. In the revolting language of those self-help books, Sybil has moved on. You know that's true. Sure, you loved each other, but you can never have that again. Just let it go."

If it had been a standard telephone receiver, Carol knew she would have slammed it down. Somehow flipping a mobile phone closed didn't have the same zing to it. She said dryly, "Thank you for that helpful analysis."

Her tone made Madeline chuckle softly. "No one understands you like I do," she said. "One day you'll have to admit that's true."

CHAPTER EIGHT

Anne met Carol as she was about to enter the comforting institutional blandness of her office. "Three things," she said to Carol, grinning.

In spite of the long hours Anne was working, her enthusiasm was unabated. Carol had to admire the positive attitude Anne had toward her punishing workload. "Well, Anne, you'd better tell me what they are."

Carrying a handful of papers, Anne followed her into the office. "First, the car's been found."

"Janet McGary's? Where?"

"Parked near a car wash in Mosman. It was polished and clean, and it looks like whoever stole it put it through the car wash, then left it in an adjacent street. An old guy rang the local police station to complain that a vehicle was parked too close to his driveway, and the attending officer recognized the license plate."

Carol leaned against the corner of her desk and folded her arms. "There won't be any prints on it — he's too careful for that. Is someone interviewing the car wash employees?"

Anne nodded. "Yes, and the people on the street where the car was parked, but I'm betting no one will remember him, even with an identikit photo to jog the memory."

"What else, Anne?"

"It's the exterminator's van." The young constable's expression became grim. "The melted plastic they found inside turned out to be a big butcher's apron, folded up. There were traces of blood. They're making a match now, but it's odds on that it'll be Sergeant York's."

An image of a faceless man carefully donning a butcher's apron to prepare for his bloody assault floated through Carol's mind.

Anne was back into her eager mode. "And we've got an envelope from the McGary crime scene." She passed Carol a sheet. "This is a photocopy — of course the original's being tested." She beamed at Carol. "They found it in the garbage can outside the back door."

"But no letter?"

"No letter."

The photocopy showed an ordinary envelope,

rather stained and crumpled. The printing was in block capitals. PERSONAL was followed lower down by, J. MCGARY and the correct address and postcode.

"Self-sealing envelope?" asked Carol, hoping it wasn't. If the perpetrator had licked the flap, he could be DNA typed.

"Self-sealing," said Anne. "I get the feeling he's too smart to make that kind of basic mistake."

Next to Carol's hip, the phone rang. Carol reached down and picked up the receiver. "Denise! How nice to hear from you."

Anne caught Carol's glance and mimed that she was leaving. Carol nodded, and turned her full attention to the exuberant voice at the other end of the line. "It's business, I'm afraid, Carol. Kemp Gray called me to say you were interested in the Reginald Ular case."

Denise Cleever was with the Australian Security Intelligence Organization — ASIO — and was the last person Carol would have anticipated calling about Reginald Ular.

"What's ASIO's interest?"

"Actually, it's a strange connection, and maybe you'll be able to make something of it."

Carol maneuvered herself around to the other side of her desk and grabbed a pen. "Tell me all about it."

"Gus Mansard, an executive of an American company, Redivo Corporation, was murdered in Melbourne in April this year. He and his family had been living in Australia for the past nine years or so."

Carol said, "I presume ASIO got involved because he was a foreign national?"

"Exactly. There's always the worry with Yanks

82

that it's international terrorism, but there was no suggestion that it was in this case. The murder hasn't been solved, and doesn't look, at the moment, as it's going to be unless new evidence turns up."

Frowning, Carol asked, "What's the connection with Ular?"

"While we were researching the case, we turned up the information that Gus Mansard had belonged to a pedophile ring for years. In fact, off the record, we were told that the reason the parent company in Boston transferred him out of the States had to do with rumors of his pedophile activities. His company wasn't going to risk a lawsuit by firing him, and apart from that little failing, he was an effective executive, so they moved the problem off shore."

"I think I see where you're going. Mansard was likely to contact Reginald Ular through the child porn Ular was peddling."

"They not only shared common interests," said Denise, "but they actually became fast friends. Mansard would often fly up to Sydney for weekends."

"Right."

Denise laughed at Carol's doubtful tone. "I suppose you're saying to yourself that this is all very interesting, but so what? Well, the word is that when Ular was arrested, Mansard was instrumental in getting him a sympathetic defense barrister, and even paid something towards the said barrister's considerable fees. And further, it was said that Mansard was willing to be a defense witness, but when the CEO of Redivo back in Boston got wind of the situation, he put the kibosh on the idea, so, with his career on the line, Mansard bailed out and left Reg Ular high and dry."

"So Reginald Ular and his nearest and dearest had every reason to be angry with this guy?"

"I gather Reg's brother, Philip, physically attacked Mansard while the trial was underway, but no charges were ever bought."

"God, Denise," said Carol. "If Mansard's murder is connected . . ."

"Indeed," said Denise cheerfully, "I think it's called Serial Killer on the Loose!"

Carol put aside the conversation she had had with Denise Cleever — there was nothing she could do until the promised files from ASIO and the Victorian police arrived.

She turned to the report on Orbe's accident that Kemp Gray had left her. What if Orbe had received a threatening chain letter before he died in the car crash? She checked his next of kin. A wife, Felicity.

On impulse she picked up her phone. Yes, Felicity Orbe would see her, any time before eight tonight, when she had a school meeting. Carol said she'd be there as soon as she could, and broke the connection. Orbe's wife lived at Hornsby Heights, on the northern edge of Sydney, and in peak hour traffic it would be a nightmare drive on the Pacific Highway. Even faced with this, Carol was abruptly filled with energy and purpose.

She called her neighbor and arranged for Sinker and Jeffrey to be fed. Of course, that wouldn't stop them trying the guilt trip when she got home, but at least she'd know that they meowed on full stomachs.

On the way out she told Bourke where she was going, then handed him the folder containing the material on the Ular murder trial that Anne Newsome had collected. "Some bedtime reading," she said. "And would you get someone to find out where the members of Reginald Ular's family are at the moment."

"Someone? Who?" Bourke gestured impatiently. "We're all flat out."

"Mark . . ."

"I know, Carol, I know." He heaved a sigh. "Jesus, Pat will forget what I look like, soon."

All the way north she turned the Reginald Ular case over in her mind. Anne had done an efficient job. She had obtained newspaper and magazine background articles as well as the accounts of the trial and sentencing. Seven or eight years ago, very few people had had a concept of the extent of the spiderweb of pedophile communications, or that there was an underground brotherhood of men who "loved" children that stretched across the world.

Reginald Ular had been defiant at his trial. Before sentencing he'd made a statement to the court, quoted in its entirety in the newspaper. Carol had read it several times, until she could almost hear the clear-eyed, handsome man in the media photographs saying the words: "I love children, I'm not ashamed of that. Nor am I ashamed that I loved Sally Ingersoll deeply, passionately, and that she returned that love, both emotionally and physically. I will always treasure that. I did not murder her. It would be impossible for me to do that to the person I loved. It was a dreadful, dreadful accident, and I have to live with that for the rest of my life. An accident, not murder. A higher court than this will judge me, and find me innocent."

Justice Granger Flint had not been swayed by this rhetoric. He gave Ular the maximum possible, life in prison, and he noted that his recommendation was that the prisoner should never have any possibility of parole.

Anne's research had turned up a magazine article on Ular's family and the impact of the trial upon them. His parents were both living and had supported him publicly, the tearful mother declaring that her son could not possibly be guilty of such a crime. The father, very photogenic with his iron-gray hair, military bearing — he had been a naval officer — and still handsome features, condemned the investigation as a witch-hunt by police who had perjured themselves in the magistrate's court at the committal proceedings and continued to lie in the criminal trial itself.

Reginald had one brother, Philip, who was seven years younger. A sister had died when she was eleven. There had been family photographs illustrating the article, and these included shots of the brothers together. Carol recalled thinking how pale and insignificant Philip seemed next to his sibling. It wasn't only that Reginald was by far the better looking of the two, it was also that he was usually portrayed laughing or involved in some extravagant action, while Philip stood watching.

And Philip would be about the right age now — Reverend Mette had said the man he knew as Jon Peterson was in his mid-thirties.

Carol swore as she missed the turnoff to Galston Road, which led to the small suburb of Hornsby Heights, the last housing before the road took a series of spectacular hairpin bends deep into the wild beauty of Galston Gorge. Carol took the next available left, and pulled over to consult her Gregory's directory. Felicity Orbe's street was only five minutes away.

As she searched for the street, she thought of Inspector Orbe's role in the trial. He had maintained, most convincingly, that when arrested and cautioned, Ular had broken down and confessed the murder to him in the presence of a junior constable, Stephen York. Then, realizing how he'd incriminated himself, Ular had recanted the confession.

Orbe's picture was featured frequently, coming and going from the court. Carol remembered him as relaxed in posture and in manner, wearing an affable smile, which disguised the essential malignancy of his character, but these photographs showed him looking grave, as though considering weighty matters. To Carol he looked smugly self-important, but, as she had heartily disliked him, even with the little contact they had had, she had to admit to herself that this animosity was probably coloring her attitude.

She found the address without difficulty, parking directly in front of it. The flimsy carport sheltered a battered station wagon. A broken rear light was held together with electrical tape, and rust had filigreed the bottom of the driver's door.

The house was fibro, painted a fading green. A few straggling bushes made a vain attempt to dress up what was basically a shabby square crate with a corrugated iron roof. The mailbox leaned at a drunken angle, and the front doorbell didn't appear to work.

Carol knocked, and the door was eventually opened by a heavy, dark-haired woman with a bitter twist to her mouth. She was wearing a loose floral floor-length dress and bright yellow plastic sandals that revealed chipped scarlet nail polish on her big toes.

"Come in," she said. "You're on the telly enough, so I would have known you anywhere." She indicated that Carol should follow her down the hall. Looking back over her shoulder, she said, "You a natural blonde? I've often wondered."

Carol kept her expression grave. "Yes, I am."

"Yeah, I suppose with those green eyes you could be." Felicity Orbe's tone indicated she still had some doubts on the matter. "Want a cup of tea? It'll be nice to talk to an adult for a change."

The living area at the back was chaos. At a glance Carol noticed toys, half-eaten biscuits, glasses with the dregs of garishly-colored drinks, and over-turned plastic child-size chairs.

"I mind other people's kids during the day to make ends meet," said Felicity Orbe with a sour smile. "Messy little buggers, and I haven't had time to clean up."

She led the way to the kitchen, which was marginally less cluttered. "Two of mine have left home," she said as she used her forearm to push clear a space on the kitchen bench, "and the youngest, Darlene, is still here. She goes to the local high school."

Carol nodded politely. "I see," she murmured.

The woman sloshed water into a battered kettle, slapped it onto a burner on the stove, and then looked around, frowning. "Got some clean mugs somewhere." She picked up two sitting in the sink and gave them a desultory wash under the tap. "These'll do. Take milk?"

"I have it black, thanks."

"Righto."

While rinsing the used tea leaves out of a stained brown teapot, Felicity Orbe said over her shoulder, "You're here about Sam, right?"

"Yes. Among other things, I'm interested in his connection to the Reginald Ular case. Do you remember it?"

"I most certainly do. I saw that Ular carked it at Bathurst last year. Beaten to death in a riot, wasn't he?" Her nose wrinkled in disgust. "Easy way out for the bastard."

Carol watched her dump loose tea into the pot and pour in boiling water. "Did you know that Internal Affairs had started an investigation into the evidence your husband gave at Mr. Ular's trial?"

"Oh, yeah, I knew, and that they were egged on by Ular's bloody brother. That's why Sam got cold feet and resigned. And it really brasses me off that Sam blew his job for nothing, because, what with Ular dying, the whole thing was never going to come to anything."

She opened a cupboard and took out a scratched biscuit tin. "Want a bickie?"

"No, thanks."

When they were seated at either end of a grubby pink sofa, with the mugs of tea and a plate of sweet biscuits established on a low table that was covered with a welter of coloring books, pieces of toys, and dirty plastic plates, Carol said delicately, "I was wondering if you thought there were any grounds at all for the investigation into your husband's part in the trial."

Her care in broaching the subject was unnecessary. "Too right, there was!" said Felicity Orbe. "Sam wanted to make bloody sure that Reg Ular never got a chance to get at any young kid again. He said the bloke was so slippery that he could have talked his way out of anything, so Sam made absolutely sure that he was nailed, good and proper."

"So Sam falsified Ular's confession."

Felicity glared irritation. "I just told you so, didn't I? Mind, I wouldn't be saying this if Sam hadn't slammed into a tree, the silly bastard."

"Before that car accident, had your husband received any threatening phone calls, or letters?"

The question seemed to amuse her. "Over the years, he got plenty of them, believe me. Stepped on lots of toes, Sam did. He never paid any attention to threats — said they were just blowing hot air."

"So he'd take no action?"

"I reckon he'd just slam the phone down, or, if some bugger was dumb enough to write, throw it away."

She looked at Carol sharply. "What are you saying? That it wasn't an accident that he ran off the road into that tree? As far as I'm concerned, some stupid fool in a truck was trying to pass him, and, if I know Sam, he put his foot to the floor. Always was an aggro driver. He'd been drinking, you know. Too fond of his bloody beer."

Carol said with deliberate vagueness, "It's just

that some things have come up that mean we're taking a second look at some cases."

"Yeah?" She cocked her head, her expression shrewd. "One of those things wouldn't be that cop killing, would it?

"There may be some connection to Sergeant York's death."

"So exactly what are you looking for?"

Carol made a decision to give information held back from the public. "We've kept this quiet, and I'd appreciate it if you didn't mention it to anybody, but it appears that someone has been sending bogus chain letters that threaten death if the recipient doesn't send copies on to other people."

"Sam didn't mention anything like that to me." Her lips crimped in a bitter smile. "Mind, Sam wasn't one for talking about business. In fact, he was hardly home, most of the time."

"I'm wondering if there's any chance that you've kept your husband's papers —"

"His papers? Hell, he wasn't as tidy as *I* am!" She jabbed her thumb toward the rear of the house. "After he resigned, Sam had big ideas of setting up his own security company. It was well on the way to going bust, of course, but it kept him out of my hair. Had a little office in a shed at the back. If you want to go through his things looking for this letter, you're welcome, but I warn you, it's a mess."

Felicity Orbe's negative opinion of her husband's tidiness was, if anything, understated. Carol took a good look at the extraordinary jumble of papers, boxes, and files that filled the little tin shed, and asked if she could send someone to look through it the next day.

"Hey," said Felicity, "For all I care, you can cart away the whole heap of rubbish."

"I'm sure there're some things you'd like to keep."

"Jeez," snorted Felicity, "I'm bloody happy he's gone, if you want to know the truth of it. Bastard to live with." She made a wide gesture that encompassed the whole haphazard collection. "Take it, lock, stock, and barrel. You'd be doing me a favor."

CHAPTER NINE

Mary Gavin's doctor refused to allow his patient
to be interviewed about her neighbor's death until he
had made a house call to assure himself that she was
up to police interrogation, so on Thursday morning
Carol found herself sitting opposite Janet McGary's
daughter, Alice, while Bourke attended the post-
mortem.

They were in the dingy sitting room of a small
cottage in Rozelle, a suburb that bordered Balmain.
The room was silent, except for the loud tick from a

heavy gilt-faced clock on the mantel and the soft mewling from Alice McGary.

The thought crossed Carol's mind that while they were sitting across from each other in matching over-stuffed lounge chairs in this mundane little room, the shattered remains of this woman's mother were being sliced, tested, measured, and weighed in a precise butchery.

"I'm so sorry, Inspector Ashton, I can't seem to stop crying." Alice McGary's face was blotched with red, and she looked blindly around, as though seeking some reassurance from the commonplace furniture. "I have to pull myself together. There's only me do to all the arrangements, you know . . ."

The contrast was so great between the Alice McGary that had been smiling broadly in the photograph on the grand piano and this devastated, middle-aged woman in the unbecoming brown dress, that at first Carol had to look closely to assure herself it was the same person.

"I'm so very sorry about your mother, and I know the last thing you want to do is answer questions, but it would help very much if you could do the interview now."

Almost with revulsion, Carol heard herself saying the smooth words that she employed when interviewing the bereaved relatives of victims. The woman sitting opposite her was shattered, defenseless, yet Carol would probe and prod until she was satisfied she had whatever useful information Alice McGary could provide.

Alice took a fresh tissue from the box beside her. "Maybe you wonder why I'm staying here with friends, and not at Mum's house."

She sounded as if Carol must be thinking badly of her for abandoning her mother in some way. Carol said gently, "I didn't think that at all."

"I always had my own room at Mum's, when I'd come down to Sydney, but this time . . ." She buried her face in her hands. "I thought I could stay, feel close to her, even though she wasn't there . . . but I couldn't."

Waiting for her to recover, Carol pictured the bedroom of the little terrace house. Who could place a bomb beside the pleasant face of an inoffensive music teacher and light the fuse? Had he been out of the house and away, when the explosion sounded? Or had he been audacious enough to stay and take a quick look at his handiwork?

Alice McGary blew her nose, then gave Carol a faint, damp smile. "Sorry. I'm okay now."

Opening her notebook, Carol took her through the preliminaries. She was given the history of the family — how Janet McGary had been born in Scotland, married early, and migrated with her husband to far-away Australia. Although Janet had loved children, she had had only one daughter. Carol heard how Janet McGary had been so proud when Alice had abandoned her dead-end job and enrolled as a mature age student at Macquarie University. Alice had gained a degree, majoring in English literature, and become a high school teacher like her mother.

Prompted for details about her mother's life, Alice's eyes brimmed, and she groped for another tissue. "I still can't believe it, Inspector. My mother was *loved*. She had no enemies at all. The kids she'd taught used to keep in touch long after they'd left school. And when she retired, hundreds of people were at the do the school threw in her honor. She was a model citizen — she never cheated on her taxes, she always gave to charity . . . Why would someone kill her, and in such a dreadful way?"

"Could there be any connection to your father, perhaps? I'm thinking of family or business conflicts."

"Dad? He was just a softy. Worked in the office of a moving company practically his whole life. And when he died, Mum got even more involved in the church and charitable things. She read to people in nursing homes, and twice a month she took her turn delivering Meals on Wheels."

"Did you ever meet the man who did the Meals on Wheels deliveries with your mother?"

"No, I never saw him. I think he goes to Mum's church, but I don't know his name." She sat up straight. "Why are you asking? Do you think *he* did it?"

"We just want to ask him some questions. He seems to have disappeared."

To forestall any further questions from Alice, Carol asked matter-of-factly, "Did your mother ever have any misunderstandings with neighbors or people at St. Luke's?"

"Nothing." Alice blew her nose. "Mum wasn't weak — she knew what she believed — but she didn't like friction, disharmony." She looked around, apparently wondering what to do with the collection of damp tissues she was holding.

Carol said, "So no one ever harassed or tried to intimidate your mother?"

"Of course not." She made a neat wad of wet

tissues and tucked it into the corner of the lounge chair. "There was that stupid letter . . ."

"What letter?"

"Last week, it was. Mum got this weird chain letter. I was so mad, because it upset her. Told her to throw it away, and I'm sure she did."

Chain letter. Carol was casual. "As you say, probably nothing, but can you remember when she got it, and anything about the wording?"

"It was the end of last week, I think." Alice's forehead creased in thought. "She read it to me over the phone — I never actually saw it. Started off with a quote from the Bible."

"Can you remember the quotation?"

"Yes, it's short, and Mum read it to me a couple of times — it really got to her. It was from Numbers, and it said, 'And be sure your sin will find you out.'"

Carol looked at the words she had copied into her notebook. *It's the same person,* she thought, *but what possible link could there be to Steve York?* Aloud, she said, "Can you remember anything else about the letter?"

Alice rubbed her temples with so much pressure that her fingertips left red marks. "I don't know . . . I think it had the usual rubbish . . ."

"What sort of rubbish?"

Alice became very still. She said slowly, "The letter said something about if she broke the chain . . ." She stared at Carol. "If she broke the chain she would die. I'd forgotten until now. It said she would die."

"What were the exact words? You will die if you break the chain?"

"Oh, it's impossible! It was just someone's idea of a dumb joke . . ."

Somewhere in the house a phone was ringing. Carol heard a muffled voice answering it, then footsteps approaching. Alice's friend, a similarly mildfaced woman, put her head around the door. "Inspector Ashton? I'm sorry to interrupt, but you're wanted on the phone."

It was Anne Newsome. As soon as she heard Carol's voice, she blurted out, "Janet McGary — she was on the Ular jury seven years ago! And she was the forewoman!"

"We can't find Philip Ular," said Bourke. "And he's the right age and general description."

Carol had met Bourke outside Mary Gavin's place, the witness's doctor having reluctantly decided that his patient was able to withstand the rigors of a police interrogation.

Orelia Street had returned to its sleepy normality. Wednesday's crime-scene tape was gone, and Janet McGary's place seemed just another ordinary terrace house. At the end of the street a couple of beer-bellied men stood outside the little pub laughing and drinking beer, a mother trundled a stroller along the uneven footpath, a nondescript black dog investigated the fascinating smells on a gatepost.

Exultant that at last they might have a name and a face, Carol asked, "When was Philip Ular last seen?"

"Just before Christmas last year. Apparently he told everybody he was so broken up over his brother's death that he was going overseas, possibly for years. We're checking to see if he actually left the country."

The iron door knocker was in the shape of a lion with a heavy ring in his mouth. Carol rapped sharply, saying, "Photograph of him?"

"Not so far, but he seems to have been quite an accomplished amateur actor, and had some ambitions of breaking into television. He had a portfolio that he took around to various agents, but we haven't tracked down a photo from it yet."

"It's possible Philip Ular could have obtained Janet McGary's name and address from his brother's defense attorney."

Bourke nodded, lips drawn back in censure. "Although we both know information about any juror's identity is supposed to be sacrosanct, there are always ways and means of finding out."

The door in front of them was jerked open. "You the cops?" demanded a savage voice.

"We're the cops," said Carol to the fiercely glaring little woman.

"Mary's in the back. I'm her sister, Ida, come to look after her. You mind you don't upset her more than she's upset already."

She stomped off down the narrow hallway, obviously expecting Carol and Bourke to close the front door and follow her.

Seen together, Carol realized that Mary and Ida were twins. They had the same round faces, upturned noses, rosy cheeks, and wispy white hair. Sitting side-by-side on a cane settee with striped cushions, they regarded Bourke and Carol with identical blue eyes. Apparently as a concession to the shock, Mary wore a blue dressing gown and fluffy slippers.

Carol was about to introduce herself when Mary said, "You'd better get on with it."

Ida nodded an enthusiastic assent. "Get on with it," she echoed.

Deciding that Mary Gavin's doctor had seriously underestimated his patient's resiliency, Carol introduced herself and Bourke, then asked Mary Gavin to explain what had happened the day before.

"About ten, I heard the explosion. Felt it too." She jerked her head towards the wall to her right. "Common wall with Janet's place. Thought the gas had gone. She could be a bit forgetful, you know. Turn on the stove and not light it. If it gets to a pilot light — bang. You're gone."

"So you went in next door to see what had happened?"

"Well, of course I did, young man." It was obvious Mary considered Bourke's question superfluous. "I've got a front door key — Janet and I look out for each other. So I went in, and there was smoke and stuff coming down the stairs, so I went up, fast as I could."

The animation faded from her face. Ida tsk-tsked and, putting an arm around her sister, said to Bourke. "I told you not to upset her."

"It's all right, Ida," said Mary. "They're only doing their job." She took a deep breath, and continued. "Janet was dead, there was obviously no hope for her. Head blown practically away. I felt dizzy, sick, and I went to the window for some air. It was open, and that's when I saw him going out the back way."

Carol leaned forward. "You saw someone? You didn't mention that to the officers who responded to your call."

"She was in shock," said Ida. "And her fool of a doctor gave her a sedative as soon as he got here." The next glare was for her sister. "I've told you, Mary, that man's too fond of prescribing drugs."

Carol said to Mary, "Did you know the person you saw?"

"I think so. Of course, I was looking down on him, but it looked awfully like Jon Peterson from St. Luke's. I tried to call out for him to help me, but he didn't hear me."

"Good thing," snapped Ida, "or you'd be as dead as a doornail, too."

Back in Carol's office, Bourke slumped in a chair. "Jane McGary's post was pretty rough stuff. Poor little lady, I almost felt embarrassed, seeing her lying naked while Jeff Duke cracked jokes." He gave a self-deprecating laugh. "I'm going to have to macho up."

"A cigarette on your bottom lip and a can of beer in one hand should do the trick," said Carol, knowing that he didn't want sympathy.

"At least she wouldn't have known anything about it. She was almost certainly unconscious, thanks to a whack of Valium. There was some of the tranquilizer in the house, as she had it prescribed by her doctor for high blood pressure, and traces were in the tea-pot."

"That explains how he could arrange the bomb and light it without any protest from her. I imagine he suggested a cup of tea before they set off on their deliveries, spiked the teapot with Valium, and waited until she was unconscious before carrying her upstairs."

There was a knock at the door, and Ned Cromwell leaned around the door. "Interrupting?"

"Not at all," said Carol. "As a matter of fact, I was just thinking of you."

Cromwell came all the way in, giving her a small smile. "I translate that as waiting impatiently for my report."

"Do you have it?"

"It's being typed, as we speak, but I thought you'd like the highlights."

Bourke indicated a chair. "Take the weight off your feet, Ned, and give us the benefit of your wisdom."

He sat down and arranged his feet neatly, side-by-side. "Well, people, the bomb was constructed of fifteen centimeters of white PVC piping, five centimeters diameter. It can be bought in any hardware or plumbers' supply store."

"Any hope of tracing it?"

"Not a chance. There was a fragment of the pipe that had an identifying brand, but it's available everywhere. And the two metal caps, one for each end, also are standard plumbing supplies. No luck with the fuse, the powder, or the screws and nails added to make it more deadly. Standard stuff that could be lawfully acquired any number of places, or stolen, for that matter."

"So basically," said Carol, "you're telling me you've got nothing."

"Not exactly." Cromwell looked smug. "There was

a bomb very like this used last year — same size, same mix of screws and nails added to the blasting powder. I didn't want to say anything at the scene, but once I'd checked my records I was pretty sure."

"Someone killed with a pipe bomb?" said Carol, frowning. "I don't remember that case."

"He wasn't killed — just maimed. And it didn't happen in Sydney, but way over the other side of the country in Perth, Western Australia."

"And you had records on this bomb?"

"Well, people," said Ned Cromwell with what looked very like regret, "there just aren't that many bombs in any given year." He showed his small, chalk-white teeth in a private smile. "So, in what you might call the bomb fraternity, we tend to share everything we've got."

"Who was the victim?" said Carol, prickling with anticipation.

"Carter Perles, Q.C. He's a barrister."

"I know who he is." Carol looked over at Bourke. "Carter Perles was Reginald Ular's defense counsel at his trial."

CHAPTER TEN

When Carol came back from her morning run on Friday she found Sinker waiting for breakfast with strident cries, but no Jeffrey. After a search she found him curled up under a bush in the front garden. He wasn't his usual self, but a quick inspection didn't reveal any wound or abscess — he had been known to battle for territory with cats in adjacent properties — so she carried him out to the back deck and settled him in a sheltered spot.

Before she left she called her next-door neighbor, Olga's doting owner. Jenny was an accomplished artist who worked office hours in her backyard studio to produce wildflower designs for a very successful line of greeting cards. Carol asked if she would look in on Jeffrey during the day, and call if she thought there was anything seriously wrong.

Driving the S-bends up Spit Hill, Carol wondered if she should call Sybil and tell her about Jeffrey — he was her cat, after all, and Sybil loved him dearly. Carol had thought she would ask for him back when she returned to her own house, but Sybil had said it was obvious Jeffrey got on with Sinker, plus he had all the bushland around Carol's place in which to lurk, so Jeffrey had been left in residence.

Carol opened the flap of her briefcase and fished around for her mobile phone, intending to pull over and dial Sybil's number — it wouldn't do for a police officer to be picked up for using a cellular phone while driving — but then she had second thoughts.

Maybe Jeffrey had been stalking something half the night and was just tired. And if she called, Sybil might think she was just manufacturing some excuse to see her. Carol slid the phone back into her briefcase. She'd call only if Jeffrey really had something wrong with him.

Bourke was already hard at work when Carol arrived. She surveyed his desktop, always so tidy in comparison to everyone else's, including her own. It reminded her of the pristine desk of the signwriter she had seen on Monday with Anne. It riled Carol that, however she struggled, she could never achieve such order.

"How do you do it?" she said. "We must get the same amount of material in the paper wars."

"My mum," he said. "She was a fanatic when it

came to neatness. Ironed our socks, even. Some of it must have rubbed off on me."

"You'd be an angel to live with, Mark."

He laughed. "Pat says it drives her mad."

His grin faded as he opened a manila folder set so that its bottom border was exactly aligned to the edge of the desk. "I'm sure you want an update."

"Please." Carol could see his precise handwriting marching down the first page. She looked at his bent head with affection. He was conscientious, reliable, and she trusted him implicitly.

"First, Steve's funeral is set for next Monday, ten o'clock. Full uniform, with an honor guard. It's going to be hard . . ."

"Yes." Carol thought of Lauren in black, going to the church where she had expected to be married.

Bourke pinched the bridge of his nose. "There'll be two of them next week. One of us should be at Janet McGary's service, which is set for Wednesday. Do you want me to ask Anne?"

Carol shook her head. "I'll go."

This wasn't respect for the dead, or even sympathy for the bereaved, although Carol felt both these things. It was a staple of fiction, but occasionally it did happen in reality that a murderer would attend, or at least observe from a distance, the funeral of a victim.

Carol had studied the amended artist's impression that had resulted from the session with the Mettes, and later today she would see photographs of Philip Ular. She was sure that, disguised or not, she had a good chance of recognizing him if he should come to gloat over his accomplishments.

"The final reports are on your desk about the

crime scene at Steve's house. The blood expert confirmed what Liz said about the perp taking off something that protected his clothes and shaking the blood off it, only it wasn't a raincoat, it was the big plastic apron found half melted in the van."

He sighed. "And, of course, the blood traces on it matched Steve." Looking up at Carol, he said, "You know, I still can't believe that he won't walk through the door over there and say it's all been a big mistake."

"I know what you mean." A platitude, but she did know. It was fanciful, but for Carol the death of someone so vital and dynamic left traces in the air, echoes of energy that whispered like a well-remembered voice.

Bourke said, "And the Mansard files from ASIO and Melbourne have arrived. They're on your desk, too." With a wry grin, he added, "You're fighting a losing battle, Carol. You'll never get it as tidy as mine is."

"I'd better go and look at them."

He put up a hand. "Not so fast. I've got more. The envelope found in the rubbish at Janet McGary's was posted locally. Mass-produced stationary. No usable fingerprints, no saliva. And her car was clean. Again, no fingerprints, no fibers, no nothing."

"He's careful."

"Sure is. The Terror of Insects van was stolen in Queensland three weeks ago. Just disappeared from a secondhand dealer's yard one night. And we found nothing in it, either."

"Philip Ular plans well ahead," she said with grudging admiration. "And he's thorough."

"So you're positive it's him?"

"Looks like it. I'm taking Anne with me to interview his parents when she can get them to agree to a time. I haven't any illusions that they're going to be cooperative — you know they refused to provide a photograph of Philip yesterday — but there might be something there. It's worth a try."

He closed his folder. "One last thing. I've got Ferguson out at Felicity Orbe's place going through the papers in the back shed looking for a chain letter. I can tell you, he's complaining bitterly. Says he's never seen such a mess in all his life." A smile flickered for a moment. "Ferguson's also found a nice line in pornographic literature."

"What sort?"

"Relax, Carol. Sam Orbe liked big, busty girls in surprising poses, doing even more surprising things. All consenting adults. No kids."

Carol stretched. It was going to be a long day. As she turned to go, Bourke said, "And Mrs. Perles called back a few minutes ago. She will grant us an audience at precisely ten-thirty this morning."

"An audience? I gather she sounds formidable."

"Old money," said Bourke with a wise nod, "and lots of it. That can make anyone formidable."

"Not only does Margaret Perles comes from the rich, landed gentry," said Bourke to Carol as he navigated the traffic on New South Head Road, "if you add to that the stiff fees that Carter Perles, Queen's Counsel, extracted from the well-heeled accused he defended, you have a fortune to play with."

"Somehow I don't think he's enjoying it much, now."

108

Carol's dry tone brought an affirmative grunt from Bourke. Changing lanes to avoid a lumbering bus spewing clouds of diesel exhaust, he said, "Perles might have any number of disgruntled clients after his blood, because he failed to keep them out of the slammer. Reginald Ular was hardly his only failure."

"You're saying it's a coincidence that the fore-woman of the jury and the defense counsel are both blown up with similar pipe bombs?"

He grinned at her. "Playing devil's advocate." Sobering, he added, "If we add Steve to the list, that's three down, and how many to go?"

"Possibly Sam Orbe and maybe Gus Mansard, the American friend who dumped Ular when the going got too hot."

"Jesus, Carol, if you're right, that's five people. Four dead, and one half dead."

"And we don't know how many more Philip Ular has in his sights."

"Charming thought," said Bourke, smoothly swinging off the main road into the exclusive streets of Vaucluse. "But this morning I've got Mills picking up several photos from an acting friend of Ular's, so we can plaster his face all over the media. We won't have to wait long until someone identifies him."

Carol wasn't as sanguine as Bourke. Philip Ular had prepared very well for his campaign against the people he blamed for his brother's death. After an-nouncing he was leaving Australia, he had authorized his father to sell the Canberra X-rated video business his brother had signed over to him after the trial, and then Philip had liquidated all his other assets. Considerable cash in hand, he had disappeared, re-emerging, it seemed, in the roles he had prepared himself to play: pest exterminator for Steve York; parishioner of St. Luke's and Meals on Wheels driver for Janet McGary.

There was a chance that both Inspector Orbe and Carter Perles would be likely to recognize Philip Ular from his attendance at his brother's trial, so Carol thought it unlikely that he would play a part that would bring him close to either of them. He was an accomplished actor, however, so perhaps he might consider it worth the risk. Even now, he might be close to someone else, watching and waiting for the opportunity to strike . . .

"Ever been to Vaucluse House?" asked Bourke, breaking into her thoughts.

"I'm not sure. Why?"

Bourke pointed to the right. "Very historical. It's a street or so that way. I had dim memories of a boring school history excursion, where we all dutifully trooped through the place with people shouting at us not to touch anything."

"And I'm sure you didn't," said Carol. "I always imagine you as very law-abiding."

"Well, of course," he laughed. "Anyway, two weeks ago Pat dragged me there again. You know, I'm just a blank cultural slate for her." He made an amused face at Carol. "You'd be astonished how knowledgeable I'm becoming, what with the art and architecture and all. For instance, I bet you didn't know that Vaucluse House was rebuilt in the eighteen-thirties in early Gothic Revival style."

"You're right, Mark," said Carol, "I didn't know that."

"Speaking of mansions," said Bourke as he drew

up beside granite gateposts, "I believe we're about to visit one."

Although the gardens were bursting with gorgeous blooms and the lawns were green carpets sweeping down to the blue-green of Sydney Harbour, the building that squatted in this beauty was not comely. Capping its two stories of gray stone was a low-pitched slate roof that sprouted many bulky chimneys. Two awkwardly shaped cast-iron balconies embellished the facade. The front door was outlined by painted metal columns and decorative plaster ornaments.

Bourke frowned at the edifice. "Now, Pat would know the architectural style . . ."

"Try ugly," said Carol.

An Asian man in a tailored white jacket and black pants opened the door to them, nodded when Bourke said who they were, and ushered them inside. Wearing white canvas slip-on shoes, he moved silently, but Carol and Bourke's heels clicked on the dark red tiles of the wide hallway as they followed him toward the back of the house. As they walked Carol caught a glimpse of marble fireplaces and lavish furniture in the rooms they passed.

Still without a word, the man halted at one door, opened it, and gestured them through into a sumptuously furnished lounge room. "Detective Inspector Ashton and Detective Sergeant Bourke," he murmured, before turning silently on his heel and exiting.

"I'm Mrs. Carter Perles," said a woman as she rose gracefully from a divan, offering her hand to Carol for a moment, but ignoring Bourke. Gesturing toward open French doors, she continued, "I thought we could sit outside. Bonnie will be bringing us refreshments."

Impeccably dressed in a beige suit and a high-necked white silk blouse, she was cool, patrician, and very straight of back. A string of pearls complemented her pearl earrings, and she wore a clustered pearl ring on her right hand. Although Carol estimated she was in her mid-seventies, her skin was only lightly lined, and the delicate honey-blond tint of her hair looked almost natural.

Her eyes flicked over Bourke, and then she evaluated Carol. Knowing that her own expensive suit and discreet jewelry passed muster, Carol smiled to herself as she wondered what the woman would think if she knew that Carol had a miniature automatic nestling in a holster under her well-cut jacket.

"This way," said Mrs. Perles. The patio was deeply shaded by ornamental grapevines that hung in heavy loops from white crossbeams. Mrs. Perles indicated that they should seat themselves at the table, which was made from a huge slab of roughly finished wood, balanced on thick fence post legs. The chairs, each one individual, were similarly massive.

"Made from a country shearing shed," said Mrs. Perles, indicating the furniture. "It was on one of my family's properties and well over a hundred and fifty years old when it was demolished."

A maid, complete in black uniform and tiny white apron, appeared with a huge tray, which she slid onto the broad table with one skillful movement. Mrs. Perles dismissed her with a nod.

She remained standing, surveying with approval the silverware and china cups on the tray. A matching china plate held thin whitebread sandwiches, cut into small triangles. "Tea? Or perhaps coffee, Inspector? And help yourself to cucumber sandwiches."

"Black coffee, thank you."

Mrs. Perles didn't speak to Bourke, but indicated with an look of inquiry that he could nominate his refreshment.

"Tea, thanks," he grinned. "With milk and lots of sugar."

A faint flick of an eyebrow showed her disapproval, though Carol wasn't sure if it was Bourke's cheerful tone or his preferences that occasioned Mrs. Perles's displeasure.

Accepting the delicate china cup, Carol said, "As I told you on the phone, Mrs. Perles, our present investigations have indicated some possibility that there may be some tie to your husband's case."

Mrs. Perles passed a cup to Bourke and indicated to him that he should use silver tongs to help himself to the sugar cubes in a silver bowl.

As she seated herself, she said, "Carter will be joining us, Inspector, but I do hope that you realize that he is quite unable to answer any questions in a meaningful way. I'm sure you're aware that he sustained devastating head injuries in the explosion, and he barely recognizes family members. Recalling details of the past is therefore quite beyond him. Also, I'm afraid he has been much worse lately, although the doctors are not sure why this is so."

Carol had read the medical summation of Carter Perles's physical condition. In one moment Carter Perles had been transformed from a respected elder member of the New South Wales bar to the wreckage of a human being. He had lost one eye, most of the fingers of his right hand, and hearing in both ears had been seriously affected. Worse than this, however, was the destruction the explosion had dealt to his brain. His skull had been cracked like an eggshell, and the tender structures of his cerebrum forever blighted.

"You were in Perth when it happened," said Carol.

"That is so. As is our custom every year, we were visiting Western Australia to spend Christmas with my daughter and her family. It was to be only for a week, but in actual fact we were there for several months while Carter recovered sufficiently to travel back home to Sydney."

"I know this must be upsetting for you, but would you mind going through the details for us?"

Mrs. Perles gave Carol a chilly smile. "Upsetting? That's a very inadequate word, Inspector. And the fact that the authorities have been quite unable to bring anyone to book for this grievous assault makes the situation even more disturbing. I agreed to see you in the hope that perhaps you have some new information that might lead to the apprehension of the creature that did this."

She turned her cold glance on Bourke, who had taken out his notebook. "This conversation is off the record. I do not chose to be interviewed; however, I will cooperate to the best of my ability, in the hope that it will assist in arresting a suspect in the near future."

"We've had a case with a pipe bomb very like the one that injured your husband," said Carol.

Alert, Mrs. Perles said, "Indeed? With a similar fuse?"

"Yes. The victim was drugged, and the bomb placed in close proximity."

"Carter was not drugged. He simply had had a heavy Christmas luncheon with the appropriate wine and a good port to follow."

The police report, delivered by courier from Western Australia, had contained crime-scene photographs of the plush study where the bomb had exploded. At the conclusion of the Christmas dinner Carter Perles had excused himself from family entertainments and had gone into his son-in-law's study, apparently to have a doze in one of the maroon leather armchairs. His daughter had looked in on him and seen him sleeping.

A few minutes later, someone had come into the room, almost certainly through the floor-length windows that opened directly into the garden. The intruder had placed a pipe bomb on the table next to the sleeping Perles. The fuse had been lit, and the person had disappeared back into the garden.

It seemed that something had roused Perles, as the pattern of injuries indicated that he had turned away from the table where the bomb was sitting before the explosion occurred. Reading the report, Carol had wondered if he had waked, opened his eyes to the unbelievable, stared at the bomb for a moment, then tried to get away. Whatever had impelled him to move, it had saved him from death.

"Here's Carter, now," said Mrs. Perles, standing as though greeting someone whose company was keenly awaited. A white-coated attendant pushed a wheelchair through the French doors and onto the sandstone patio. The man in it was slumped to one side, his mouth drooping open, his one eye staring straight-ahead. The right side of his face was misshapen and the bald skull dented. The tight skin was a shiny red. One of the hands relaxed in his lap was whole, the nails manicured, an expensive gold watch on the wrist. The other hand was a ruin, lacking all digits but the thumb and little finger.

"Thank you, Paul. I'll call you when I need you." The slight, dark man inclined his head, then retreated soundlessly on thick-soled white shoes.

Carol looked at the wreckage of Carter Perles, Q.C.

This was enough revenge for you, wasn't it? Perhaps better than death.

She said, "In the case we're investigating at present, the victim received a threatening letter the week before the attack."

Mrs. Perles was fussing about the positioning of her husband's chair at the table. Bourke half rose to help her, but a glance was sufficient to dissuade him from offering assistance. Satisfied with the arrangements, she poured a cup of tea and positioned it near her husband's good hand. "Carter," she said gently, "drink your tea."

He looked at the cup, then at her face. With a clumsy movement he reached toward the table. She helped him take a mouthful, then dabbed at his lips when some of the liquid dribbled down his chin.

Seated again, she said to Carol, "A successful defense barrister will often get hate mail from people who imagine that he has obfuscated the truth to the jury and thus allowed a guilty person to escape justice."

"And unhappy clients?"

"If they were found guilty, then they *were* guilty. My husband was an excellent advocate, but even he couldn't work miracles. No one had any cause to doubt his dedication to his or her case."

Bourke said, "Do you remember a man called Reginald Ular? Your husband defended him nine years ago."

She gave a minimal shrug. "I don't recall that name. I paid very little attention to Carter's work, although, of course, I fully supported him. He knew that the details of criminal law were often distasteful to me, so we did not discuss them."

Carol had a strong conviction that Mrs. Perles knew that her husband had devoted a disproportionate amount of his career to the defense of individuals accused of crimes against children. Perhaps it was just because word of mouth about his abilities had drawn pedophiles to seek his legal services, but there was a reasonable possibility that he himself, if not a pedophile, was at the very least a sympathetic fellow-traveler.

The man in the wheelchair made a guttural sound. He knocked his hand against his cup, overturning it in its fragile saucer. "Ahhh," he said.

Mrs. Perles rose swiftly to mop up the tea with a linen table napkin. "It was just an accident, Carter. Don't worry yourself. I'll get you another cup."

Watching him closely, Carol said, "Perhaps Mr. Perles remembers Reginald Ular . . ."

The man's one eye swiveled toward her. His

mouth opened and closed, but he made no further sound.

Pity rose like bitter bile in Carol's throat. Whoever he had defended, and for what accusation, did Carter Perles deserve this?

Then she thought of the countless children brutalized, their bodies and minds corrupted, their trust destroyed.

"The particular threat to your husband may have come in the form of a chain letter," she said, watching Carter Perles face.

He blinked, then slumped back in his chair.

"A chain letter?" Mrs. Perles creased her brow. "I'm not altogether sure what that is."

Bourke gave a succinct description. She waited until he had finished, then said to Carol. "I don't remember anything like that, but of course I didn't see every item of mail that Carter received."

"There may have been a quote from the Bible included in the letter."

"The Bible?" said Mrs. Perles. Her mouth tightened. "Have you noticed how the ignorant are drawn to quote biblical texts? It seems to them, I imagine, that it gives some sense of legitimacy to their beliefs."

"Could you look in your husband's papers to see if perhaps he did receive such a letter?" Carol asked.

A look of displeasure indicated that Mrs. Perles was not happy with this blunt request. "I have hired someone to put Carter's papers in order before I commission an author to write my husband's memoirs. If such a letter exists, Ralph will have seen it."

"If we can speak with him, Mrs. Perles, we can

describe exactly what he should be looking for," said Bourke.

"I'm afraid that is not possible. Ralph is taking a short vacation at the moment."

A sudden chill touched Carol. "Sergeant Bourke will show you an artist's impression of a man. It may be someone you have seen recently, or in the past."

Mrs. Perles didn't take the sheet but left Bourke holding the illustration for her to examine. A shadow of surprise crossed her face. "Why," she said, "that could be Ralph Phillips."

CHAPTER ELEVEN

"Okay, everyone," said Bourke, whiteboard pen in hand, "to bring you up to date..."

He waited while someone who'd come in late to the lunchtime briefing found a chair. There was a feeling of anticipation in the room, and from her position beside Bourke, Carol looked around at the familiar faces of her colleagues with a recognition that, to a person, they would work long hours, do anything and everything that was necessary, to find Philip Ular.

Photographs of the suspect had been obtained

from one of his friends, and everyone in the room had several blown-up versions of his face, together with a detailed description.

Philip Ular was thirty-five years old, 180 centimeters tall, and of slim build. He had brown hair, fair skin, hazel eyes. His face was unremarkable, with even features and a pleasant expression. In one photograph he smiled widely, his eyes crinkled in apparent delight. An ordinary, agreeable man in his mid-thirties: a monster who killed without compunction.

Bourke rapped the whiteboard, and the murmur of conversation in the room quieted. "Reginald Ular, convicted murderer, dies in a prison riot in November last year just before the legal machinery for the consideration of a new trial grinds into action. Then, in mid-December, Inspector Samuel Orbe is run off the road and killed near Wyong, New South Wales. That one's officially still an accident, but Orbe was Reginald Ular's arresting officer and he testified against him at the trial."

Anne, who was sitting in the front, said, "The truck that sideswiped Inspector Orbe had Queensland plates, and we know the suspect later stole the van that was used in Sergeant York's murder from Queensland. Maybe he makes a habit of getting his vehicles interstate."

Besides Anne and herself, there was only one other woman in the room, Maureen Oatland, an experienced officer who had worked for years in what had once been regarded as "women's work" — rape and juvenile crime. A total of three out of twelve was better odds than usual. Carol had read recently that women made up only 14 percent of police officers in

New South Wales, although the latest batch of probationary constables sworn in at Goulburn Police Academy had a higher proportion of females.

"Next on the list," said Bourke, "Carter Perles is blown up with a pipe bomb last Christmas Day in Perth, Western Australia. Critically injured, but not killed. Now he's pretty much a vegetable in a wheelchair. He can't talk and has trouble communicating in any way. He was the barrister who defended Reg Ular, and he obviously failed to keep his client out of jail."

Carol broke in to say, "This morning we interviewed Mrs. Perles. She made a tentative identification of the artist's impression we had of the suspect, saying that it could be the man she recently hired to put her husband's papers in order. We haven't been able to trace him, but he gave the name of Ralph Phillips."

There was a buzz of comment at this: it was common for suspects to use the same initials, or variations of their names when making up pseudonyms. *Ralph Phillips* used Philip Ular's first name with the addition of an extra letter, and also one of his brother's initials.

Bourke tapped the whiteboard again. "In Melbourne, April this year, Gus Mansard, an American national, was shot outside his home. He was a top executive in Redivo Corporation, and the company, as a matter of course, provided him with a permanent bodyguard. The gunman disabled him, then shot Mansard to death."

"What's the connection to Ular?" asked Bryant Mills, a constable relatively new to the unit.

"Mansard was a friend of Reginald Ular's and, it

appears, a fellow pedophile. He was to appear as a witness for the defense, but he got cold feet and withdrew not only his testimony, which had to do with the loving relationship he claimed to have observed between Ular and his schoolgirl victim, but also the considerable financial support he'd been providing."

"Why the three-month gap between Perles and Mansard?" Ferguson asked. Carol made a mental note to ask him how he was going with the material in Sam Orbe's shed.

Bourke shrugged. "We don't know, but it may be the planning required to carry out the murder. There's another four-month gap until Steve York is killed."

"Let's get the bastard!" from someone at the back was followed by mutters of angry assent.

"That was last Sunday," said Bourke. "On Wednesday Janet McGary, who had been the forewoman on Reginald Ular's trial seven years ago, was killed with a pipe bomb that resembles closely the one used to maim Carter Perles."

"Those gaps," said Mills, "maybe during that time he was killing other people we don't know about yet."

It was a thought that had occurred to Carol, too, but it would take time to compile a list of individuals concerned with a trial so long ago. Grimly, she considered the fact that Philip Ular had had years to polish a killing list that could be activated in the eventuality that his brother failed to win release.

The brothers must have been very hopeful of gaining a new trial, particularly because of the revelations of corruption in the police service and the ominous cloud that hung over the reputation of the inspector who had testified to a verbal confession that Ular denied ever making. To come this close, only to have Reginald die violently in prison — Carol could imagine the grief and rage that Philip must have felt.

Carol said, "Thank you, Bryant, that's an excellent point about other possible victims. Some of you will have the task of making a list of likely targets and tracing their present whereabouts. We don't know how Philip Ular's mind works, so we can't be sure how he selects his subjects for revenge. It will be a lot of work, but these people have to be warned."

"On that subject," said Bourke, "we know that in the last two cases, the York and McGary murders, Philip Ular had close contact with his victims. In Steve York's case, he posed as a pest exterminator who was offering a free examination for white ants. The trouble he took over Janet McGary was even greater: he became a parishioner of St. Luke's, Balmain, for several months, even volunteering to help her with her Meals on Wheels deliveries. And now it looks as if Ular managed to get into Perles' house as a secretary of sorts, although it's not clear if he was there to gloat or if he intended to finish the job and kill him."

"He's as game as Ned Kelly," said Mills, his tone close to admiration.

"This isn't a heroic bushranger standing up to the troopers," Carol snapped. "Philip Ular is a serial killer who's possibly murdered, at last count, four people, and crippled one. And I hardly need remind you that Steve York was one of the victims."

Mills looked abashed. "Yeah, sorry . . ." he mumbled.

The meeting broke up after Bourke assigned individual tasks. Carol stopped Ferguson on his way out. "How are you going with the papers in Orbe's backyard office?"

"Office? You have no idea what's in that shed. It's like the inspector took every bit of paper he'd collected over the last twenty years or so and shoveled it into one little room. I'm about halfway through, but I haven't found anything to do with the original Ular case and certainly no chain letter."

His shoulders drooped. "I'm going back there this afternoon. I don't suppose I could have any help?"

"You can ask Mark, but I don't think we can spare anyone else."

"I see."

Bill Ferguson's hangdog look amused Carol. "Is Felicity Orbe being cooperative?" she asked.

"Oh, yeah." He rolled his eyes. "Along with countless cups of tea, she's given me a blow-by-blow of her life with Inspector Orbe — what a no-hoper he was as a husband, etcetera, etcetera."

"Watch out," said Bourke, overhearing the end of the conversation. "She might be on the lookout for a replacement. A fine young man like you . . ."

Carol went back to her office and checked her diary for the next few days. She'd spoken to the security company that employed Gus Maynard's bodyguard, Wyatt Riggs. Riggs was now working in Sydney, and he had agreed to come in tomorrow

125

morning, so she had to wade through the files on the American's murder before then.

Philip Ular's parents had resisted all Anne Newsome's attempts to schedule an appointment, and finally Carol had called herself and pinned Malcolm Ular down to the next day, Saturday, at their flat in Clovelly.

Steve's funeral was on Monday morning, and she was dreading it. The ceremonial farewelling of a police officer, the pallbearers in uniform, the honor guard . . . She had never cried in public, and wouldn't on this occasion, but she knew it would take tight control to prevent it.

And Janet McGary's funeral was on Wednesday.

So many individuals slaughtered to appease a vengeful rage. As Carol leaned back in her chair, the little Glock nudged her in the small of her back. *She* had some protection against attack: Out there were people who had no idea that they were even targets.

She had decided to release information about the contents of the chain letters to the media in the hope that anyone receiving one would contact the police. Maureen Oatland was in charge of the team researching everyone involved in the Ular trial. Perhaps, even as they worked, Philip wore some innocuous disguise, smiling at his next prey, ready to strike again.

The ASIO and Victorian police files on Gus Mansard's death sat on her desk, waiting. She spent the rest of the afternoon reading and making notes, sustained by mug after mug of black coffee. She always meant to bring in her own ground coffee, and every now and then she did so, but pressure of work usually meant that she forgot and had to consume the evil-tasting brew that fueled the department.

She had just closed the last folder when the phone rang. "Carol, it's Jenny. I've just been in to see Jeffrey, and he's much, much worse than he was this morning when I called in to check on him. He's really sick, and my daughter's borrowed my car, so I can't take him to the vet for you."

"I'll be right there."

She broke the connection, then dialed Sybil's number. There was a good chance of getting Sybil at home, as she was only teaching part-time and had Fridays off.

As soon as she heard Sybil's voice, Carol said in a rush, "Jeffrey's very ill. When he was a bit off-color this morning, I asked Jenny next door to check on him, and she's just called to say he needs to see a vet and she hasn't got her car . . . I don't know what's wrong with him . . . Okay, I'll probably make it before you do, so I'll pick Jeffrey up and meet you at the vet's. Would you ring and say I'm bringing him in?"

As she drove she pictured Jeffrey's ginger face and fat furry cheeks. He was demanding and cocky, but a tickle under his white chin reduced him to a pliant purring machine.

A pulse of rage shot through her. Could he have been poisoned? She could kill a person who set baits for animals. Well, perhaps not kill, but seriously beat up . . .

Carol smiled wryly. So who was she? A sworn police officer, or a vigilante?

Jeffrey was fully as sick as Jenny had said. She

met Carol at the carport, carrier in her arms. "He's in here, Carol. He needs a vet fast."

Jeffrey was lying on his side, panting. His eyes didn't focus on Carol, but he growled halfheartedly when she opened the wire door of the carrier to look at him.

"Thanks, Jenny. I'll let you know what happens."

As she drove into the veterinary clinic's parking lot, she saw Sybil's red hair as she opened the waiting room door. She had obviously just arrived.

My love, thought Carol. She eased the carrier out of the car and rushed into the clinic.

"Blocked bladder," said the vet, coming out into the now-empty waiting room. He wasn't the comfortable middle-aged woman that Carol usually saw when the cats had their shots. This vet had thick black hair, a thin, intelligent face, and a censorious manner that suggested that he considered Carol had failed in her duty of care. "Have you been feeding Jeffrey dry food?"

Carol immediately felt guilty, although she didn't think she had reason to do so. "Well, yes," she said, "but not much. And he always has lots of water."

"He's had small quantities of dry food all his life, without any problem," said Sybil, with a sideways glance at Carol to show solidarity.

"A male cat's urethra is very narrow, so it blocks easily," the vet said severely. "Jeffrey is to have no more dry food, even the special formulation. It was touch-and-go this time, but he'll be all right. I'm

128

keeping him under observation tonight, and you may ring tomorrow morning after nine to find out when you may take him home. On Saturdays we close at twelve, so if you are picking him up, it must be before that time."

"I feel thoroughly chastened," said Carol when they were outside in the parking lot. "I'm a failure as a pet owner. That vet made it perfectly clear."

Sybil laughed and patted her shoulder. "Jeffrey's always been a terrible greedy-guts. I'd say he's been stealing dry food from Sinker, from neighborhood cats — anywhere he can get it. It isn't your fault, Carol."

Suddenly lighthearted that Jeffrey was going to be okay, that Sybil was there with her, Carol said, "Come back and have something to eat. Or a drink, at least. Will you?"

"Okay."

Buoyed by Sybil's immediate agreement, Carol drove home in higher spirits than she could re-member having for some time, and when Sybil pulled in beside her in the carport, she thought, *This feels right. It's as it should be.*

Jenny had been watching for Carol's car and met them as they locked the cars. "Carol, Sybil, hi!" She gave Sybil an enthusiastic hug. "So great to see you. How's Jeffrey?"

Leaving Sybil to explain Jeffrey's medical problems, Carol grabbed the letters from the mailbox and went to open the house and turn on the lights. She wanted it to be welcoming, warm — somewhere so familiar, so comforting, that Sybil would want to stay, at least for a while.

Sinker gave Carol a subdued greeting. Ears

pricked, he homed in on Jenny and Sybil's voices, and abandoned her to pad off up the path to see them.

Carol went down the hall, switching on lights. She caught sight of herself in the hall mirror. As always, she had a jolt at the change in her face. Her nose, once subtly aquiline, was puffy, imprecise. She had become accustomed to the discomfort at the bridge of her nose when she put on dark glasses, and now automatically took care when she washed her face, but she was sure she could never get used to how it looked. Soothing words from the plastic surgeon had not convinced her that she would ever be the same.

"So? It's only a nose," she said to herself. She didn't sound convincing.

Hearing Sybil's footsteps on the path, Carol hurried through to the living room and kitchen. Dropping the mail on the counter, she glanced around. Did everything look okay? What could she offer for a meal? At least she had eggs . . .

Carol had a moment of wry amusement: she was acting like a kid trying to impress a date.

"Omelette?" she said as Sybil appeared, Sinker, tail high, behind her. "I've got eggs, cheese, and a couple of other things I could throw in."

Sybil slid onto a kitchen stool as though she had never been away. "That'd be great. Anything I can do?"

"Scotch. After our harrowing time with Jeffrey, I'm desperate for alcohol."

"You've got a postcard from Aunt Sarah," said Sybil, picking up a postcard featuring a gigantic salt-water crocodile with jaws agape. "You get all the good ones. Mine today was of a sunset from Cape York."

Carol hadn't known her Aunt Sarah was writing to Sybil, but it warmed her to know it. "Those old dames are really something," she said.

"I'll say! I can just picture the three of them bouncing along the outback roads in that minivan plastered with stickers from where they've been."

Beating the eggs, Carol found herself whistling tunelessly between her teeth. She was happy. With a shock she realized she could hardly remember the last time she'd felt so elated.

Impulsively, she said, "It makes me happy that you're here." When Sybil turned her head from the drinks she was pouring, Carol added quickly, "That's how I feel. There's nothing else implied."

"Look, Carol."

Sybil was pointing to the sliding glass door that led to the back deck. Attracted by the light, and no doubt expecting reward of food, the mother possum, bulky baby clinging to her back, had ventured right to the door and was squinting shortsightedly through the glass. On their side Sinker glared indignation, quite aware of the insulting fact that the possum didn't regard his presence as a threat.

As she cooked, Carol watched Sybil out on the deck feeding pieces of banana to the possum, with smaller chunks for the baby, who was almost large enough to fend for itself. Carol could not imagine Madeline doing such a thing. She would be amused, interested in wildlife, but not involved.

They had a relaxed meal, sipping Scotch between

131

mouthfuls of an omelette that had, by some miracle, turned out to be perfect.

"If that intimidating vet says Jeffrey's okay, I'll pick him up and bring him home here," said Sybil. "I presume you'll be working."

"Yes." With amazement, Carol realized that for a short time she hadn't given a thought to the case that consumed most of her waking hours. "Do you mind if I turn on the late news? I want to see if the media's got the story straight."

They moved into the adjacent living room, taking their coffee with them. Carol wondered if she'd sleep at all tonight, considering the caffeine overload she'd had.

The newscast on Madeline's channel was just at the first commercial break. After ads for a drain cleaner, the superior services offered by a bank, and the trailer for the latest action movie, a promo ran for Madeline's show.

"All this coming week, *The Shipley Report* comes to you from Asia, the powerhouse of the Pacific rim!" the voice-over announced, while shots of Madeline smiling, speaking to national leaders, and gazing appreciatively over scenic backgrounds rolled with a background of vaguely oriental music. "The scandals! The secrets! The Asian decisions that can affect you and yours!"

The voice finished with a triumphant, *"The Shipley Report*! The news behind the news!"

Carol glanced sideways at Sybil. "I'm not —"

"Don't say anything." Sybil's voice was mild. She didn't look at Carol as she spoke.

The news desk appeared on the screen. "Deadly chain letters," said the glossy blond woman, with a

132

smile. The three words, superimposed over a blurred envelope, appeared on the screen behind her. She grew marginally more serious as she went on, "Those that have received one of these chain letters in the mail have died horribly."

After this sensational beginning, the elements of the story were efficiently given, ending with a photograph of Philip Ular gazing seriously into the lens. "Police say that this man, Philip Ular, may be able to help them with their inquiries. He could be using another name. If you believe you have seen him, please contact the police at this number."

As the contact number flashed up on the screen Carol had the disheartening thought that thousands of spaced-out individuals with a tenuous grip on reality would be reaching for their phones at this very moment, convinced that they knew the man in the photograph.

"I taught the little girl that his brother killed."

"What?" Carol could hardly have been more astonished. "Sally Ingersoll?"

"Yes, poor little thing."

Carol stared at her. "I never knew."

Sybil raised her eyebrows. "Why would you? It was years ago, before I met you. I was teaching at a high school over the other side of the Harbour, and Sally was in my Year Seven class."

Skin prickling, Carol said, "You didn't have anything to do with it, did you? The trial, I mean."

"No."

Relaxing, Carol breathed, "Thank God for that."

"I was going to be called as a witness for the prosecution, but at the last moment they decided they didn't need me."

"As a witness to what?" She waited for Sybil's answer with growing alarm.

"Actually, I think I was the first person to blow the whistle on Reg Ular. As you know, teachers are protected from legal action when they report even a suspicion of child abuse. Poor little Sally . . ." She shook her head. "Oh, Carol, when I think what she must have gone through . . ."

"So you went to the principal and said you thought Sally was being sexually abused?"

"Yes. I said I was sure she was, both from her behavior and some of the things she'd said. She'd mentioned the photographic sessions with the next-door neighbor, and I'd got his name from her. I had to put in a written report, of course, and then the machinery swung into action, but you know what bureaucracy is like — Sally was dead before they did anything constructive." She looked down at her hands. "I've always wondered if I could have done something more . . ."

"Darling, you could be in danger." The endearment Carol had been avoiding slipped out. Sybil didn't seem to notice.

Carol went on, "We haven't released the details, but we have every reason to believe that Philip Ular is stalking, and killing, people he blames for his brother's guilty verdict."

"He can't blame me. I wasn't a witness at the trial."

"The defense would have been given the full prosecution witness list. If there was a possibility you were going to be called, you would be on it. Besides, Reg Ular would know very well who had reported him."

"Carol, I haven't received a chain letter, if that's what you're worried about. And believe me, I'd tell you like a shot, if I did." She smiled reassuringly at Carol. "I don't think there's a chance that he'd be interested in me. I mean, there's the judge, there's the jury . . ."

"Janet McGary was killed on Wednesday. She was forewoman on Reginald Ular's jury."

There was an obstinate set to Sybil's mouth. "I'm not going to worry about it. I not only live in a different suburb, after all this happened I married, and changed my name. He couldn't find me if he wanted to. With his photo everywhere, you'll catch him in a day or two, I'm sure."

The best persuasive talents Carol could muster failed to convince Sybil that she should temporarily move residence, or take any other evasive steps, such as driving a rental car instead of her own.

Walking in the moonlight up through the garden to the carport, Carol said, "Call me if you have the slightest worry. If anything's strange, or out of place. Even if it's something you think is silly or unimportant. Promise me you will."

Sybil stopped at the gate. "It's not necessary, but I promise." She laughed softly. "Does that satisfy you?"

"It'll have to."

They looked at each other for a heartbeat, then Carol leaned forward and gently kissed her on the lips. *No demands. No ownership,* she thought.

Carol resisted putting her arms around her, so their lips were the only point of contact. The kiss was soft, sweet. She felt dizzy with the desire to show Sybil how different things could be, if only . . .

135

Carol broke away first. She stepped back. "Drive carefully," she said.

"I will."

Carol stood watching the red rear lights of Sybil's car until she turned the corner and was out of sight. Sinker came purring to wind himself around her ankles.

"Maybe there's a chance," she said to Sinker. "But I'm not hoping too much." As she said that, she knew she might be.

CHAPTER TWELVE

Saturday morning was like a regular weekday. The media release of the photograph had set the phones ringing constantly with reports that the suspect had been seen in widely separated places, such as a tour bus on the way to Broken Hill, pumping petrol in a local garage, hitchhiking on the road to Wollongong and — Bourke's favorite — working as a disk jockey at a Sydney radio station.

All the tips that weren't obviously from disturbed people had to be followed up, but Carol was sure that, even though the photograph released to the media was more tangible than an artist's impression, Philip Ular would have faded into the background as he had after each hit.

Carol sat with Maureen Oatland going through the list of possible targets from the trial. It included the magistrate at the initial hearing who had found that Reginald Ular had a case to answer, the crown prosecutor, members of the jury, and witnesses, particularly those who testified against the accused.

She got on well with Maureen Oatland. She was a big woman in every way. Physically large, though not overweight, she had a loud, penetrating voice and an astonishing appetite for junk food of every type. "Never met a hamburger I didn't like," she was fond of saying.

This morning it was doughnuts. She had every possible variety crammed into a large cardboard box, which she offered to anyone passing. Maureen had looked with scorn at Carol's selection of a plain sugared doughnut. "Chocolate's much better. Or custard-filled. Or jam. Raspberry jam's good."

Carol had quickly skimmed the list of witnesses Maureen had compiled, and hadn't seen Sybil's name. Knowing she could have missed it, she asked, "Is this a complete witness list, including those who weren't called to testify?"

"I've culled the names from the transcript of the actual trial," said Maureen, "so it only includes people who actually got up in court." She took a large bite of a pineapple doughnut of noxious yellow. "Why would he waste time on people who didn't testify, when he's got enough to keep him busy with those that did?"

"How are you doing with locating them?"

"It's amazing how people can disappear over a period of seven or so years," said Maureen. "So far I've only found a couple of the jurors, although I've got the judge — that is, I know where he is. Justice Granger Flint's retired from the bench and he's overseas at the moment. No word of when he's coming back."

"Inspector, there's a personal call for you," called one of the officers in the main area.

Carol went into her office, hoping it was Sybil to say that she had picked up Jeffrey.

"Carol Ashton."

Madeline was mock indignant. "Bloody inconsiderate! You wait until I get out of the country to break a terrific story!"

"You make it sound as if I did it on purpose, Madeline."

"Well, you can make it up to me by giving me an inside run. You won't regret it, Carol, I promise you. Do we have a deal?"

Madeline Shipley's husky voice was often amazingly successful at coaxing people to do or say things they didn't intend. Carol had seen politicians, usually wily, let down their guard and, as a result, find themselves skewered on television.

"No deal," she said.

"I'll be home soon, and then I'll find a way to persuade you," laughed Madeline, not at all discouraged.

They talked for a few moments more, but Carol refused to be drawn on anything, personal or official, and eventually Madeline, still cheerful, rang off.

She checked her watch, then rang the veterinary clinic, to be assured that Jeffrey had spent a comfortable night and could go home.

The next call was from Sybil to say she had just spoken to the clinic and was picking Jeffrey up before twelve. She would take him back to Carol's place and fuss over him a little.

"You've still got your key?" said Carol. "Jenny has one if you don't."

"I've still got my key."

Carol found herself smiling. "Good," she said.

They said casual good-byes. Carol still had her hand on the phone when it rang again.

"I found it!" Ferguson was triumphant. "The chain letter. Inspector Orbe had shoved it between the pages of a book on running small businesses."

"Have you got the envelope?"

"Yes."

Carol could hear Felicity Orbe saying something in the background. Ferguson went on, "There's no reason for me to stay here now." The relief in his voice was palpable.

"Come right in," said Carol, smiling. "And that's an order."

Ferguson obviously took her literally. He was there in a much shorter time than it had taken Carol to drive to Hornsby Heights on Wednesday night. He handed her the letter and the envelope, each in a clear plastic sleeve.

"It was folded up in the envelope when I found it, like he'd read it, then shoved it back in."

Carol read the letter, holding it so Bourke could see it too. "Well, Mark, now we know what the body

140

of the chain letter is like. The quote obviously varies from person to person."

Bourke tilted the plastic sleeve and squinted at the white page. "Looks like an inkjet printer to me."

Unsigned, it read:

TO WHOM IT MAY CONCERN

Whatsoever a man soweth, that shall he also reap.

You are a chosen one. Your name has been selected to receive these instructions.

Follow them exactly and you will have great good fortune. Fail, and this letter will bring you death.

Do not break the chain.

Within forty-eight hours you must copy this letter and send it anonymously to ten other people. Wonderful things will begin to happen for you within two weeks.

If you do not do this, you will die.

You have forty-eight hours. Do not break the chain.

Bourke picked up Carol's Bartlett's *Familiar Quotations* and began to flip through the index. "Here it is." He found the quote in the body of the book. "Whatsoever a man soweth, that shall he also reap." It's from the Bible. Galatians chapter six, verse five."

Watching Ferguson take the letter and envelope off for analysis, Carol said, "I don't imagine there'll be any fingerprints, except for Sam Orbe's."

"Of course not," said Bourke. "Although we don't need them, do we?"

"There isn't one bit of solid evidence to tie Philip Ular to these murders. We've had tentative identifications based on an artist's impression, and now that we've got photographs, some of the people who have met him have said they think it's the same person. They just *think*, Mark. Philip Ular has a generic face, and it's clear he subtly alters his appearance each time. Any good defense lawyer could present a convincing argument that it was an unfortunate resemblance."

"Of course it's him." Bourke was impatient. "He's got the motive that connects the killings. Once we find Ular, we'll find evidence to nail him. It doesn't matter how clever he is, he'll have made some mistakes."

He flicked the corner of a photo of Philip Ular that lay face up on Carol's desk. "This is an example — he collected all the photos he'd had taken for his acting portfolio, but he forgot a friend had a set."

"This friend was no help otherwise?"

Bourke shook his head. "I interviewed him last night. He actually knew very little about Philip Ular from the personal angle. He's a nice guy, name of Bob Rule, and another would-be actor. He and Philip met a couple of times at different auditions, and got talking. When they had bit parts in the same stage play, they rehearsed their lines together. Philip left a copy of his portfolio photos with him because Bob had a possible introduction to a well-known theatrical agent, so Bob told Philip that if he got the chance, he'd put in a good word for him, too."

"Did he know any of Philip's other friends?"

"Ah," said Bourke, "now that's interesting. Bob Rule got a bit uncomfortable when I asked that question, and I finally got it out of him that he had met some other friends of Philip Ular's, all male, and that he had felt there was something odd about them."

Carol raised an eyebrow. "They were trying to recruit him?"

"More trying to find out if they had common interests," said Bourke sardonically. "When Bob Rule tumbled to the fact that they were obliquely referring to sexual relations with children, he ran a mile."

"Did he see Ular again?"

"Yes, at an audition, but nothing was ever said about what had happened. This was November last year. Then Philip disappeared."

He stretched his mouth in a smile that didn't show his teeth. "When he didn't see him again, Bob Rule thought that he'd just given up the idea of becoming an actor, but we know different, don't we?"

Carol snatched up her phone halfway through the first ring. "Okay, I'll send Mark out to get him."

She put down the receiver. "Wyatt Riggs, the man who was Gus Mansard's bodyguard, is here."

On his way out the door, Bourke said, "I don't know who he's guarding now, but with his track record I'd feel a little nervous."

After Gus Mansard's murder in April, his family, a wife and two daughters, had returned to the States. Carol had read the wife's statement, which was of no help — she had noticed nothing wrong, knew of no threats, and couldn't imagine who might want to hurt her husband.

The man Bourke brought back with him was

143

powerfully built, but gone to fat. Thick-waisted and broad-shouldered, he stretched the seams of freshly pressed jeans and a white short-sleeve shirt. His hair was cut very short, and he was good-looking in a blunt, tough way, although his features were set in a scowl.

Riggs stalked into Carol's office as though he were a fighter about to start a round. He looked around with a pugnacious glare, then centered his gaze on Carol. "You want to see me about Maynard? Right?" He slapped a business card down on her desk. "My card."

"I'm Carol Ashton." She extended her hand, and, as she expected, he crushed it in a hard grip.

Bourke moved to lean against the windowsill, arms folded, a faint smile on his face.

Riggs had hardly seated himself before he said, "Look, I did everything right!"

Carol turned the red business card around in her fingers. *Karlyle International Protective Services* was in heavy black type. His name, Wyatt Riggs, appeared in the bottom right hand corner, followed by *Southeast Asia Region*.

"Your company specializes in executive protection, Mr. Riggs?"

He swelled belligerently, as though she had asked something aggravating. "We handle personnel security for some of the biggest international companies. So?"

Bourke blew out his cheeks. "So I don't imagine a certain international company was very pleased with your company's services."

"Shit!" Riggs was obviously disgusted with this provocative statement. "Redivo Corporation hasn't anything to complain about."

"You were responsible for Mr. Mansard's safety," said Carol. "What went wrong?"

Riggs leaned forward, resting his elbows on his heavy thighs. "Look, Carol, speaking as one professional to another . . ."

Carol avoided looking at Bourke, sure that he was hiding a grin. "Yes?" she said.

"You *need* executive protection in places like Colombia or New Guinea or Cambodia. But Australia . . .Jeez, you'd think it'd be pretty safe. I mean, it's not center stage in a world sense, is it?"

"So you let your guard down?"

Riggs swung his crew-cut head in Bourke's direction. "No way, mate. Took all the standard protective steps."

Carol didn't want to waste too much time with Riggs. When she'd spoken to the director of Karlyle's Australian operations, he had filled her in with details of the protective services provided to Redivo executives worldwide, mentioning, as he did so, that Redivo was a company rated as low-risk because the corporation produced safety equipment, not some politically incendiary product.

Also, although the Karlyle director avoided putting it in so many words, Carol had got the impression that Riggs had been taken from more challenging assignments in potentially violent countries and placed in the relative backwater of Australia because he wasn't quite up to handling some of the more volatile situations.

She had a niggling pain behind one eye that presaged a headache, and Riggs's manner was irritating her. She said briskly, "Please itemize the steps you took to secure Mr. Mansard's security."

145

Riggs splayed the fingers of his left hand and tapped the little finger with his right forefinger. "Standard stuff. First, no fancy, expensive car." He tapped his next finger. "Second, no publicity, especially photos or TV coverage."

He frowned heavily. "He *was* on television the weekend before he died, but I couldn't help that." Riggs was aggrieved. "Mansard's frigging company was sponsoring the golf tournament, wasn't it?

He tapped another finger. "Third, in restaurants I made sure he sat away from the entrance and where he couldn't be seen from the outside." He paused, if daring them to interrupt, then resumed. "Fourth, be unpredictable. Vary your routine, the vehicles you use and the routes you take."

Bourke grunted. "Someone knew where and when to get Mansard, so that didn't work, did it?"

Riggs bristled. "Look, mate, the guy insisted on using his bloody Merc, didn't he? And he didn't take any of this security stuff seriously. He'd tell anyone where and when he'd be somewhere." He shook his head. "Bloody amateur."

Carol twirled her gold pen in her fingers. "But you were the professional," she said.

Riggs jabbed a thick forefinger in her direction. "Don't try and blame me for this one. It was a terrorist attack. There was nothing I could do."

Carol consulted the report on her desk. "Part of your job is to be alert for any indication that someone is watching your client —"

"No one was. I know my job."

Bourke scratched his nose. "Well, someone sprayed you with pepper spray when you opened the car door, belted you over the head, and then shot Mr. Mansard in the face. Are you suggesting this person just happened along at the very time you were due at the security gate at the bottom of the drive?"

Riggs leaned back in his chair. The flesh of his bull neck bulged over his collar. "I've never lost one before," he said. "It's not a good feeling."

He ran a hand over his face. "We got slack, both of us. Mansard had been here in Australia for nearly ten years. I took over the assignment eighteen months ago." He shot a look at Carol. "Replaced a woman, actually. That's how easy Karlyle thought the job was."

"You know of no threats recently?" asked Carol. "Letters? Phone calls?"

"Nothing."

"How about disgruntled employees? Had Redivo fired anyone lately? Are there any lawsuits brought by staff pending?"

Riggs shrugged. "You'll have to check with the company, but I don't think so. Redivo's a pretty straight company."

"Would you tell us what happened that night, please."

"Jesus Christ!" He glared at Carol. "How many times do I have to go through it, eh? You've got it all in the report in front of you."

Carol gave him a brief smile. "Humor us, Mr. Riggs."

He sighed elaborately. "Oh, all right. Mansard was a guest speaker at a big convention on industrial safety held in the center of Melbourne. I had his Merc waiting near a side entrance, and we left around midnight. We gave a lift to another Redivo executive who was visiting from the States — dropped

147

him at his hotel about twelve-fifteen. Then we drove home. It took about twenty minutes." He rolled his eyes. "I don't see why it matters what time it was."

"No one followed you?"

"Look," he snapped at Carol's mild inquiry. "I'm trained, right? No one followed us."

"Was there much traffic?"

Bourke's question aroused his ire. "The usual amount for that time of night. I turned into our street. No one followed me in a car, and there was nobody walking around. It's a quiet neighborhood, and people mind their own business. Besides, they go to bed early."

Riggs paused and looked from one to the other, but when neither Carol nor Bourke spoke, he went on, "Okay, so I stopped at the gate at the bottom of the drive. There's a remote control in the car to open it, but nothing happened."

"And you didn't think anything was wrong?" asked Bourke.

"I would have, except it had happened before."

Carol leaned forward. This wasn't in the report. "What do you mean?"

"A couple of times the week before the gate hadn't opened. It was during the day, and I got out and did it manually. I thought the electric motor had had it, and told the guy who does odd jobs around the place that someone should look at it. Of course, the lazy bastard hadn't got around to doing anything about it, so I just assumed the bloody thing was stuck again."

"You didn't see anyone, or notice anything unusual, other than the fact the gate wouldn't open?" Bourke asked.

"Look, mate," he bristled, "if I'd seen anything unusual, I'd have had the car out of there bloody fast, I can tell you."

"I'm sure you would," said Bourke.

Riggs subsided. "Like I said, I'd got a bit slack. If I'd been in Algeria or Pakistan . . . Well, I just open the driver's door, and out of nowhere I get a glimpse of movement, and then the pepper spray hits me right in the eyes."

"You were armed?" asked Carol.

"Look, it all happened so fast. Christ, I can tell you it hurt. I was blinded and I'd got a lungful of the stuff, and I couldn't breathe. I think of my gun, but then the bastard hauls off and hits me with something hard, and I'm on the ground and out of action."

"Did the assailant say anything?"

"I'm dizzy. I can hear, but like everything's a long way away. There's a shout from Mansard, two shots, really close together, then footsteps. Then nothing. Down there on the ground, trying to breathe, I knew he was dead, and I was bloody lucky not to be."

Carol turned over a page in the report. Except for the mention of the earlier trouble opening the entrance gate, Riggs's account followed his official statement. "You say here that you're sure it was one person and that you didn't hear a car start up afterward."

"Right."

With a slight smile, Bourke said, "Could the assailant have been a woman?"

Riggs gave an incredulous laugh. "A woman bring me down? I don't think so." He shook his head violently. "It's bad enough it happened. If it was a woman . . .Jeez!"

Carol handed him a photograph of Philip Ular. "Have you ever seen this man before?"

"Nah." He handed it back, then paused. "Give us another look."

He frowned over the photograph. "Christ," he said. "This could be the guy I mentioned — you know, the one that did the odd jobs around Mansard's place."

CHAPTER THIRTEEN

"I can't help thinking," said Anne Newsome as she edged into the Oxford Street traffic, "about how that guy, right now, is probably talking to his next mark. Maybe he's playing the role of a plumber, or someone who does odd jobs. Whatever, it must make him laugh to himself to know we have no idea where he is."

Carol put on her dark glasses against the glare. "And I don't suppose he'll be obliging enough to continue sending chain letters as an early warning."

"We'll get copycats," said Anne. "There'll be chain

letters flying in all directions promising death and dismemberment. And of course, there's the Internet ... The mind boggles where this could end."

When they had left the office, calls were already coming in from people alarmed by ordinary chain letters they had received in the mail, even though the worst threats they contained were vague promises of bad luck if instructions to pass the letters on weren't followed. It seemed that merely hearing the words *chain letter* on the news triggered a panic response in some people.

Along Oxford Street, through the suburbs of Darlinghurst and Paddington, pedestrians played chicken with drivers, perching precariously on the median strip, or darting, lemming-like, through the moving vehicles. It seemed to Carol that the warm spring Saturday had brought everybody outdoors.

She sat back and tried to imagine herself into Philip Ular's mind. His behavior was sociopathic but, in his terms, rational. Intellectually, she had an understanding of the motivation that had driven him to kill — he wanted those he believed responsible for his beloved brother's imprisonment and death to be punished in the most savage way. But Carol recoiled from the cold viciousness that could so logically plan and execute the destruction of the people he blamed. It chilled her to consider what he must have been thinking as he played the roles that brought him into his victims' lives.

How could he have murdered Janet McGary, after seeing firsthand what a sweet, good woman she was? A bomb was a dreadful weapon, and he had used it twice. With a shudder of revulsion, Carol thought of Carter Perles, helpless in his wheelchair, looking into the face of the man who had maimed his body and blown his life to pieces. She had an image of Ular teasing Perles with the knowledge of who he was and why he was there, knowing that there was no way the barrister could convey the horror of what he was experiencing.

If she were Philip, who would she have at the top of her list? The judge? The crown prosecutor? The other members of the jury? Or Sybil? Carol was still nagged by the worry that he might target Sybil because she was the person who had started the dominoes falling by reporting a case of suspected sexual abuse.

But wasn't Justice Granger Flint the key player? The judge was the one who had sentenced Reginald Ular to life in prison, after trenchant comments on the depravity of his crime. The judge had also given a written recommendation that the prisoner never be released.

Sure that Philip would want to punish the man who had so condemned his brother, Carol had instructed Maureen Oatland to concentrate on finding out exactly when Justice Flint intended to return to Australia.

"We're here." Anne broke into her thoughts. Expertly backing into a tight space at the curb, she said, "It's that white monstrosity across the street."

Malcolm and Justine Ular's flat was one of many in a bloated structure with stained off-white walls. The general air of neglect it had was repeated in the neighboring blocks of units in this part of Clovelly. The Pacific Ocean and three beautiful surfing beaches

— Bondi, Bronte, and Coogee — no doubt packed with sun worshipers, were only a short distance away, but everything here seemed dispirited and sullen.

September's spring hadn't brought buoyant optimism to the area. Dusty bushes on the verge struggled to flower, succeeding in putting out a few inadequate blossoms. A daisy bush sported fatigued flowers. Leggy geraniums grimly survived in a window box.

The bright sunlight emphasized the grimy reality, but Carol felt the welcome heat and smiled. She wished that she were spending her Saturday where she could see and hear the blue-green sea smashing in breakers on the sand. Sybil's place would be ideal. They could walk down to the beach, buy an ice cream, walk along the edge of the foam . . .

"It's at the back," said Anne Newsome, pointing to a laconic sign that held a faded red arrow and numbers. It directed them to follow a narrow concrete path that ran down the side of the building if they wanted UNITS 16 TO 30.

The fat building next door seemed to lean over them as they passed into cool shadow. Through the many open windows came a cacophony of sound: loud voices; children crying; music blasting; someone practicing on a drum set; a man yelling "Bitch! Bitch!"

"Nice, quiet neighborhood," said Anne, grinning. "Reminds me of my student dorm."

Number sixteen was on the ground floor at the end of a dim, grubby corridor. The door had frosted glass panes in the top half, and when Anne pushed the cracked white bell button, almost immediately a face, distorted by the glass, appeared. "Who is it?" asked a tremulous female voice.

Anne gave their names. The face disappeared. There was a long pause. Anne had her finger poised to ring again when another form swam into view through the rippled glass. "Who is it?" This time the question was demanded in deep masculine tones.

Anne went through her routine again. The door opened abruptly. "I want to see some identification."

"Mr. Ular, I'm Inspector Carol Ashton."

Malcolm Ular was taller than she had expected, but he had changed little from the press photographs she had seen. His thick hair had faded from iron-gray to almost white, but the planes of his face were still well defined. He stood rigidly, his shoulders back and his feet together. He wore dark pants and a pale blue short-sleeve shirt, both with the crisp appearance of clothing recently ironed.

He looked Carol up and down. "Yes, I know you." His tone did not indicate any pleasure at the recognition. His glance moved to Anne. "You, Missy. Who are you?"

After examining Anne's identification, he waved them inside. "Down there. First on the left."

The small sitting room had a fireplace that had been converted to hold a two-bar radiator, although the thick dust on the coils made Carol wonder if it had ever been used. The chocolate-brown couch and matching chairs were massive, half filling the area. A small electric fan on the mantel turned from side to side, sighing to itself as it tried to whip up a breeze in the stale air.

"I suppose you'd better sit," said the man grudgingly. He gestured toward the robust couch, then raised his voice to demand, "Justine, come in here."

A woman's head came around the edge of the

door. Malcolm Ular gave an impatient click of his tongue. Thus impelled, Justine Ular brought the rest of her body into the room and slithered onto the nearest brown chair, whose size almost overwhelmed her slight form. She smoothed her olive-green skirt over her knees and, ignoring Carol and Anne, fixed her gaze on her husband, who stood with his back to the fireplace, his hands behind him.

"Well?" he said to Carol. "Get on with it."

"When did you last see Philip, Mr. Ular?"

He answered without hesitation. "Why, that would be January this year. Before he went overseas." Casting a flat look in his wife's direction, he added, "You agree, don't you, Justine? January?"

"Yes, January."

Carol repressed a sigh. This was like wading through treacle. "There's no record that your son left the country. In fact, we believe that he is still in Sydney. Has he contacted you in any way?" A pause, filled by the whisper of the little fan. "Ms. Ular? Perhaps you have spoken to him recently?"

"That's *Mrs.* Ular," said her husband.

Anne flipped over a page in her notebook, the sound loud in the silence that followed his remark.

Tentatively, Justine Ular cleared her throat. "Philip," she said in her reedy voice, "I saw his picture on the television and in the paper this morning. You think he's done something dreadful, don't you?"

Deciding that polite sparring was a waste of time, Carol said, "We would like to question Philip about a series of murders. We believe he may be able to help us."

Justine Ular bent her head toward her lap until

Carol could see the pink of her scalp through her lank graying hair. "It's about Reg," she whispered.

Thinking how unsuitable a strong name like Justine was for such a wispy, ineffectual woman, Carol asked her, "Did Philip ever talk about revenge, after his brother died?"

Malcolm Ular took a step forward. "Revenge? How about justice? There are some that say that those that put Reginald away should be castigated."

A pulse of anger hardened Carol's voice. "Mr. Ular, I have read the transcript of your elder son's trial. He was convicted of murdering Sally Ingersoll. Evidence was given that before her death he had sexually abused this twelve-year-old girl over a period of many months."

"I believed my son when he told me it was an accident." There was color in Ular's cheeks, and Carol had a sudden impression of how extremely good-looking he must have been when young. His voice strong with conviction, he continued, "Reg was no murderer, and he didn't deserve to be bashed to death by degenerates in prison. I hold those that sent him there fully responsible."

"What Reg did was wrong." Justine Ular's voice was almost inaudible.

He turned his head. "What did you say?"

She didn't look at him. "Nothing." She shrank back into the chair, compressing her lips into a thin line. It was clear she had withdrawn from the interview.

Carol continued to press Malcolm Ular about his younger son, but her questions were deflected or ignored. Finally, hiding her frustration, she ended the interview. Carol hadn't expected much, but she had hoped to gain at least a little information about Philip Ular's activities and the names of some of his friends.

"Hell's bells," said Anne when they were back in the car. "Like getting blood out of a stone."

"It may be that they actually know very little."

"Oh, I think Justine knows something, and she'll tell us, sooner or later." Anne's lips curved in a satisfied smile. "I slipped her one of my cards — even wrote my home phone number on the back. Her husband's such an absolute bully, I'm sure she'd love to put one over on him." Her grin widened. "Do you want to bet money on whether she calls?"

"You didn't tell me Jeffrey had plumbing problems," said Bourke accusingly when Carol returned. "Sybil called for you, and when she got me, she told me all about it."

"Is he okay?"

"I'd say Jeffrey is fine. He's got Sybil with him, patting his paw. She says she'll wait at your place until you get there, or take him back home with her if you're going to be very late."

"Thanks, Mark, I'll call her."

Bourke lingered for a moment, as if to say something more, then he gave her a smile and left. He was very fond of Sybil, and Carol knew that he was wondering if there was any possibility they might get back together again. He would never say anything directly on the subject, but on other occasions he had made it clear, obliquely, what he thought.

It was both comforting and exciting to hear Sybil answer her phone. Carol could picture her in the kitchen in her characteristic pose, leaning back against the breakfast bar, ankles crossed, gazing absently out at the gumtrees lining the deck.

"Are you in the kitchen?" Carol asked.

"Nope. In the bedroom. Jeffrey is insisting that he needs a king-size bed to recover fully. I made him a comfortable nest in a cardboard box, and put it in the living room, but he won't stay there."

"I'll be home by eight. Is that too late?"

She found herself holding her breath for Sybil's answer.

"That's fine. I'll order pizza, shall I?"

Maureen Oatland, yawning, came into Carol's office as she was preparing to leave. "I've had it," Maureen said. "Do you have any idea how many people swear they've seen Philip Ular today?"

Carol gave her a sympathetic smile. "Quite a few, I imagine. But one of them may have. That's the problem."

"Yeah, well, I'm here to do a progress report." She slumped her substantial body into the nearest chair. "I've found eight of the jurors so far. Two are dead . . ." She put up a hand before Carol could respond. "Natural causes. I checked. The others have been warned that a homicidal maniac may be after them. None of them seemed particularly alarmed. And fortunately, no one's received a chain letter, or anything like it."

"How about the trial judge?"

"Next Wednesday," Maureen said. "That's when Justice Granger Flint returns to these fair shores."

Carol slid a file into her briefcase. "How did you find out?"

Maureen stifled another yawn. "Sorry, must be the hours I'm working. I finally contacted Flint's sister-in-law. He's a widower, and since he's retired is always jazzing off on cruises and whatever."

She laughed as she added, "Julia — that's his sister-in-law — thinks he's looking for a new wife, and she doesn't altogether approve."

Carol asked, "So where is Flint now?"

"On a cruise ship off New Zealand, lucky bastard. He should be safe enough on the high seas."

"It docks in Sydney?"

"Wednesday, three o'clock."

"I want someone on the ship with him before anyone else gets on or off."

Maureen pursed her lips. "We could arrange to go out on the pilot's boat when the ship comes through the Heads."

"Do it."

"It could be wise," said Maureen, running her hands through her hair. "As it turns out, I wasn't the only person interested in the judge's arrival details."

Carol put down the manila folder she was holding. "What do you mean?"

"While we were chatting, Julia just happened to mention that someone else was very interested in the judge's whereabouts. When this guy rang — she couldn't remember the name he gave — he said he was with the Law Society, and needed to know for some honorary dinner they were planning for Justice Flint."

"She told him?"

"Yes. Why wouldn't she? Seemed quite aboveboard to her."

Carol sat down slowly. "Of course you checked with the Law Society."

"Of course I did. No dinner. And they didn't give a damn where Granger Flint might be."

Playing with her black opal ring, Carol said, "What's been happening with his mail while he's been away?"

"Ha!" Maureen was complacent. "I thought of that, too. Seems Julia's been collecting it every time she goes to water the plants in the judge's penthouse. She opens anything that looks like a bill, so she can pay it, and puts the rest in a pile."

"Maureen, I have no doubt you asked her to check all the envelopes."

"I did. She's down the coast tomorrow, watching a polo match, would you believe, but she promised to go through the mail on Monday. I told her if she sees anything faintly resembling a chain letter, not to handle it, but to ring us."

"Good work." Carol stood, and picked up her briefcase. "I'm out of here. You should be, too."

"You know," said Maureen reflectively, "I don't know if it's occurred to you, but we could use the judge" — she gave Carol a wicked smile — "for bait."

CHAPTER FOURTEEN

"It's important to differentiate between *spree* killing and *serial* killing."

He stroked his gray goatee with a soft, white hand. "Of course, in this case, I would term the Chain Letter Killer an *early warning* murderer, which is a subgroup of the serial killer genus."

With polished admiration the interviewer said to the camera, "Evan Lewdale is a world-famous expert in the criminal mind and author of *Killer from the Cradle*."

She turned to him with a practiced smile. "Now,

what can you tell our viewers about the Chain Letter Killer?

The screen switched to a close-up of Lewdale, who looked suitably professorial. "As I demonstrated in my book, *Killer from the Cradle,* I believe a serial murderer is born, not made."

Leaning over Jeffrey — as resident invalid, he was ensconced on the couch between them — Carol took another wedge of pepperoni pizza from the tray on the coffee table. "I just knew he'd get a plug in for his blasted book," she said.

Sybil chuckled at the note of disgust in Carol's voice. "Have you met the great man himself?"

"Lewdale? Fortunately, only once, at some function I had to attend. As I remember it, he tried to give me some pointers about appearing on television."

"You? The media princess?" said Sybil mockingly.

Carol laughed. "That's right! The hide of the man!"

"So Lewdale isn't a criminologist?"

"Not a criminologist's bootlace. He's managed to become a media expert on crime without any formal training or even familiarity with policing."

Jeffrey gave a plaintive cry. Sybil said severely, "No, you can't have any pizza. You're on light rations, cat."

Lewdale was saying authoritatively, "It's in the wiring of the brain, mainly. In a killer of this type, faulty circuits overload and the individual's behavior goes quite outside normal societal parameters."

The interviewer nodded enthusiastically. "So the Chain Letter Killer was born bad?"

He inclined his head in stately agreement. "Indeed."

"And what do you, as an expert, make of the letters?"

Carol gave a snort of derision. "Not much, I'd say, since he hasn't even seen the text of one. Lewdale just knows what the public does — that it's a chain letter than threatens death, and it starts with a quote from the Bible."

On the screen, the expert was posing self-importantly. "Letters," said Lewdale to the expectant face of the interviewer. He paused, tugging his beard with the appearance of one deep in thought. "Threatening letters, using biblical quotes."

"Yes, what do you make of that?" Carol demanded of the screen. She caught Sybil's sideways glance and grinned. "Sorry, I get carried away when a fool like this sets himself up as an authority."

"Why haven't *you* done your usual media briefing?" Sybil asked. "I keep on expecting to see you on the news, but you never feature. Why is that?"

"Because Ular is what you might call a selective murderer, we pretty well know his targets, so a general warning wasn't necessary. The superintendent decided that circulating the photographs and the information about him was good enough. Besides . . ." Carol touched her nose. "I don't want to expose this to the television cameras more than necessary."

"You are *so* vain, Carol," Sybil laughed. "It looks fine to me."

"Religious mania is a potent force," Lewdale was intoning. "The human psyche yearns for spirituality, but this yearning can be turned to darker purpose. It is obvious that this murderer has been brought up in an intensely religious household and has no doubt been forced to do penance for sins, imagined and real —"

He blinked out of existence as Carol hit the power button on the remote. "That's as much as I can stand," she said.

Sybil reached for her coffee. "Why *is* Philip Ular sending these letters?"

"I don't believe for one moment that it's religious mania," said Carol, inspecting the remaining slices of pizza and deciding against eating any more. "Frankly, I think that it is simply that it amuses him. And it's a demonstration of his power, because he can warn his victim in advance yet still carry out the execution. And in the case of someone like Janet McGary, there's a possibility that she actually discussed the letter with him. Can you imagine how intoxicating that would be? To know you were going to kill someone, and that she, all unsuspecting, is talking to you about the threat?"

Sinker came stalking in from the deck. He glared at Jeffrey on the couch, then walked over to butt his head against Sybil's leg. He arched his back as she ran a hand over his spine, then moved on to Carol for a similar acknowledgment.

Sybil said, "I know Philip Ular is obsessive about his brother's death, but how that can be enough motivation for what he's doing?"

Carol lifted her shoulders. "Who can really understand? We had a psychological profile drawn up by a genuine expert, not a charlatan like Lewdale, and basically she said that Ular totally believes that he's entitled to exact revenge for a profound and devastating wrong. In his mind, these killings aren't murders, but justifiable retaliation for what was done to his brother."

"That's quite a list."

"And you're on it." Carol's tone was blunt. "I wish you'd take the situation seriously."

Sybil scratched Jeffrey between his ears. He lifted his chin and purred when she stroked his throat. "Ular's got quite a few people to go before he gets to me."

"We don't know how he's allocated blame. It might be that you're near the top of his list of candidates because you were the first to report the abuse of Sally Ingersoll."

"Carol, I've told you. He can't find me."

Grabbing the tray with the remains of the pizza, Carol stood. "He can find you, if he wants to. You worked as a teacher for the New South Wales government. That means the Department of Education has you on its computer files. Believe me, it's not hard to get information."

Jeffrey made a pathetic protest as Sybil left his side. Gathering up the mugs, she said, "Jeffrey, you can't play sick tyrant very much longer. The vet says you're okay."

Joining Carol in the kitchen, she said, "I don't think Philip Ular would even remember I existed. I was just a little cog in the machinery of justice."

"Picturesque imagery," said Carol tartly, "but I think you're wrong. Philip Ular is vitally interested in anyone who had a hand in putting his brother away. And he doesn't have to go to that much trouble to find you. He can say he's a friend who taught with you, and ask around the school you were at seven years ago. Apart from records, there are also teachers who stay at one place for a long time. Someone will know your married name and your present address."

Leaning against the bench, Sybil crossed her arms protectively. "You're frightening me."

Carol swung around and put her hands on Sybil's shoulders. "Good," she said gently. "Then maybe you'll take sensible precautions."

Staring into Sybil's eyes, Carol thought, *If anything happened to you* . . .

She had a vision of the first time they made love, remembering the desire that had vibrated between them, the breathless need to assuage the body's craving. It had seemed so important, so overwhelming then. Now she saw how simple and uncomplicated that relationship had been. What shoals and reefs they had negotiated since then.

"How do you do this to me, Carol?" Sybil's smile was rueful.

"Do what?"

Sybil shifted restlessly, and Carol dropped her hands.

Shrugging, Sybil said, "I had it all worked out. Thought it through, and realized that we'd outgrown our relationship."

"You're being kind." Carol kept her tone light. "*You* had outgrown the relationship. You made that quite clear before you left for London. I was the one who was quite happy with the status quo."

"Yes, I do remember saying something along those lines." Sybil shook her head. "I'm so angry with you."

"Angry? Why?"

167

"I had everything under control. I knew what I was going to say and how you would react. I'd thought it through — I didn't sleep all night — and you're so physically exciting, Carol. I knew it would be easy to let that sway me, but I wasn't going to let it get in the way."

Sybil moved around the kitchen, touching things, picking them up and putting them down. Carol watched her, silent because she was apprehensive that something she might say or do might destroy the tenuous communication between them.

"I hate it, Carol, when I've got some measure of peace about something and then it starts to blow away."

"I don't want to make it hard for you."

Sybil gave a soft laugh. "Yes, you do, Carol."

"All right. I admit I want to make it hard for you to dump me and easy for you to stay."

"Dump you?" Sybil spread her hands. "I believed everything was cut and dried. I'm happy without you, I say to myself, and it's true, Carol, it's true. Then, when I tell you it's over, and you are so reasonable, it kills me."

"On Wednesday? *You* killed *me*."

"I was so sure you'd argue with me," Sybil's tone was aggrieved. "So sure you'd use that bloody self-assurance that indicates that you know what's best for me, always." She tilted her head, exasperated. "But you didn't react the way I expected you to."

Not sure what to say, Carol asked, "Where are we now?"

"I honestly don't know."

Meowing weakly, Jeffrey came into the kitchen. He sat down, ears slanting at a pitiful angle. "You ham," said Carol, stooping to stroke him.

She looked up at Sybil. "Stay the night, please."

When Sybil didn't reply, Carol added, "Stay for Jeffrey, if not for me."

"Carol . . ."

"You could sleep with Jeffrey."

"He'll be at the end of your bed."

"I know."

Sybil looked down at the floor. "I don't know why I'm even considering . . ." She raised her chin. "All right."

Turning the lights off, Carol said, "I suppose you learned a few things in London."

"I suppose I did."

For a moment, Carol felt the sting of resentment for whoever it had been who had shared Sybil's bed. But how could she feel jealous? She'd hardly been celibate herself.

Carol showered, mind in neutral, not wanting to anticipate, to set any limits, rehearse any moves. *Desire is cheap and easy to satisfy,* she thought. *This is something different, all consuming.*

She felt that she would be hungry forever if she couldn't find some way to keep Sybil in her life. On any terms.

She could hear the shower in the second bathroom. Carol got into the bed, and lay, waiting.

Jeffrey came in, inspected her, and left, languid tail waving.

Carol closed her eyes and drifted. She seldom read

poetry, but strangely, Emily Dickinson's words coalesced in her mind: *Wild Nights — Wild Nights! . . . Might I but moor — Tonight — in Thee.*

She smiled at her caprice. Sybil would chuckle if she knew that Carol was quoting a poem to herself.

"Get out of bed, Carol, and come to me."

She opened her eyes. "Have ever words had more eroticism?"

Standing by the door, Sybil opened her arms. "Will you come?"

It was a solace to take those few steps across the room. "You are my harbor," she said.

Sybil laughed, surprised.

She felt the heat rising from Sybil's skin. Fingertips traced the lines of Carol's face, collarbone, nipples, stomach, thighs.

Carol thought, *This is an affliction for which there is no cure.* Not meaning to, she said, "I love you."

So easy to kiss that eager mouth, hear the hammer of heart, the scent of skin. Sliding her lips over throat, shoulders, holding her tight and secure.

Sybil's arms about her, evanescence in her blood, music singing in her ears. How could she have forgotten how right this was? How they fitted together, patterned for each other, complete and whole?

"Sybil, I feel —"

"Stop talking, stop being gentle with me."

They were on the bed, kissing wildly, turning together, breast to breast, skin to skin — the axis, the center, the focal point of all desire.

Down, down, deep down. *How do I love thee, let me count the ways . . .*

Carol could shout for joy as her body rang in the liberty of effortless relief.

She woke much later. Moonlight fell across the tangled sheets. Jeffrey was curled neatly at the end of the bed. Sybil murmured and turned to throw an arm across her. Carol smiled, and went back to sleep.

CHAPTER FIFTEEN

A light mist of rain was falling when Carol set off on her run, Olga bounding at her side. It was Monday, the morning of Steve York's funeral. Running easily, Carol enjoyed the haze of moisture against her skin. As she entered the bushland reserve, delicious, elusive scents rose from the wet ground. Olga was in ecstasy, softly yipping to herself as she chased smells to ground, showering herself with droplets from the wet undergrowth until her fur was saturated and she had to stop and shake herself with whirligig enthusiasm.

Carol jogged to a stop at the edge of a high sandstone cliff overlooking Middle Harbour. Curtains of rain rippled across the surface of the gray-green water, an up-gust of air swept the fragrance of damp eucalyptus leaves into her face.

To be alive on such a morning.

Tears filled her eyes. Today she would wear black for Steve.

Before she left for work, she punched in Sybil's number. "Good morning." She avoided any endearment. Their new intimacy was too fragile to burden it with any suggestion of proprietorship. "I just called to say I'd like to see you soon."

They agreed on Tuesday night for dinner. Carol stood for a moment, looking around the kitchen. Sunday morning they had made brunch together, relaxed, but wary not to push emotional boundaries. Then Sybil had gone home to her house.

As she left, they had kissed good-bye, lightly, a memory of passion quivering between them.

"Careful, I'll be very careful," Sybil had said when Carol repeated her worries about her safety. "I know what Philip Ular looks like, Carol. I'd recognize him in an instant. I guarantee he isn't lurking in the neighborhood, pretending to be a tree lopper, or something like that."

Carol had already put in a request for the local police to have a patrol car check Sybil's house at regular intervals. Short of having a surveillance team in place — and she had nothing concrete to justify that — she had to hope that Sybil was correct and that Philip Ular had other quarry in mind.

She checked her black suit for lint. She'd read somewhere that white was the Chinese symbol for mourning. How strange to go to a somber ceremony wearing the color of summer and sun. Steve York was Catholic, so today he'd be buried in the dark, wet earth.

Carol left home later than usual. The rain had turned from mist into a steady downpour, and there had been a serious accident on the Spit Bridge. Carol sat in stationary traffic while an ambulance on the wrong side of the road wailed its way to the crumpled wrecks. A patrol car was already there, and several tow-truck drivers had arrived to fight over the vehicle carcasses.

Ahead she could see a uniformed officer directing traffic. Carol remembered when she had been a green patrol officer not long out of training. The first time she had controlled the movement of cars around an accident, she'd been somehow surprised and pleased that the drivers obeyed her signals.

The rain intensified, bouncing off the bonnet of the car in splintered silver drops. She moved two car-lengths, then stopped. The water drummed on the roof, the thwock-thwock of her windscreen wipers was a metronome, like the steady beat of her heart.

Digging her mobile phone out of her briefcase, Carol called in to say that she was held up in traffic and would go straight to the funeral. She was given the message that Maureen Oatland wanted to speak with her urgently.

When Maureen came on the line, her strident voice fizzed with raw energy. "Hey," she said, "just on a hunch, early this morning I went around to the posh apartments near Hyde Park where Justice Flint has his penthouse. Got talking to the building super-visor. It seems the management hired a new part-

174

time handyman recently. Called himself Ray Unwin. The supervisor couldn't speak too highly of him — said he did excellent work."

She paused, and Carol took the cue. "You showed the supervisor Ular's photograph?"

"Did I ever! And got a dead cert I.D. Would you believe, since the beginning of September, Philip Ular has been working in the building from ten to four, Monday, Thursday, and Saturday."

Stung with relief that this was proof that Sybil wasn't the next target, Carol said, "Who have we got there to arrest him when he reports for work?"

"Mark Bourke sent Bill Ferguson, but it won't do any good. The new handyman called in at seven this morning, and left a message that he'd had a better job offer, and wouldn't be in again."

Carol slapped the steering wheel in frustration. "Hell!"

A horn blared behind her, and she realized the lane of cars in front of her was moving. She accelerated. "Is Mark there?" she asked Maureen.

"He's going to Steve's funeral with Superintendent Edgar. They're about to leave."

"Make sure Mark has the address of Flint's building, and tell Ferguson to stay out of sight, just in case Ular does turn up. We'll join him there, straight after the service."

She flicked the cell phone closed and threw it on the seat beside her. The traffic ahead, freed from the bottleneck of the accident, was moving faster. Water thrown from her tires drummed against the wheel arches.

What had frightened him off? Or did he have all the access he needed? Was his plan set? Perhaps he had booby-trapped the penthouse and could sit back and wait for Justice Flint to open the door and walk in. Or was he settled in the apartment, enjoying the judge's unintentional hospitality, while he waited for his victim to spring the trap?

Ignoring the law against driving and using a mobile phone at the same time, Carol snatched it off the seat and called Maureen Oatland back. Carol tapped a rapid tattoo with her fingers until the veteran cop came on the line.

"Maureen? You said Flint's sister-in-law, Julia, was going to sort through the judge's mail today."

"Yeah. Julia Pell. She said she'd go up there some time today, but I don't know when."

"Contact her and stop her from going to the building before we get there. If you can't find her, tell Bill Ferguson to stake out the lobby. It's imperative that she doesn't go up to the penthouse. Okay?"

"Jeez," said Maureen. "It never occurred to me he might be there. Maybe that's why you're the inspector, and I'm not."

Her throat tight from unshed tears, Carol watched the pallbearers in dress uniform carry Steve's mahogany casket from the church where he had worshiped all his life. She had never thought of Steve as religious, so it was unexpected to find that he went to mass almost every day. People who had known him had got up and spoken to the packed church.

It had nagged at Carol that Steve, whom she had valued as a fine officer, had lied at Inspector Orbe's behest. There was no question that what he had done was wrong, but the parade of those who had known and loved Steve, whose lives had been touched by him, began to mitigate the distress she felt because of his dishonesty.

The rain still fell in gray sheets. The crush of people outside the church blurred into faces and umbrellas. Ubiquitous television cameras, protected by plastic hoods, recorded everything for the evening news. Carol could write the script, the shorthand that summed up human tragedies into fodder for the media.

Tonight, an announcer, suitably solemn, would intone, "Tragic funeral of a young officer, hacked to death in wedding home . . ." There would be a close-up of Lauren at the funeral, weeping inconsolably. "The bride's dreams of a life together slashed by a madman's knife . . ."

Carol turned her back on the crowd and the cameras. She had plainclothes officers seeded throughout the crowd, scanning for Ular. She spoke the empty, rote words of consolation to Lauren and to Steve's parents.

It was a guilty relief that she and Bourke would not be going to the graveside, to stand in the rain and watch Steve's body lowered into the ground. Carol had always wanted to be cremated, reduced to ash by clean fire. Not to lie rotting in darkness.

In the car, Bourke told her that he had contacted Justice Granger Flint on the ship and explained the situation. The judge had said that he would prefer to return home, rather than be off-loaded in a New Zealand port.

Bourke fell silent as Carol drove with dull precision. There was nothing more to say about Steve's life and death, or the other lives irrevocably damaged by his murder.

Secure in its exclusive affluence, the superior apartment block, faced in polished gray stone, soared complacently over the green of Hyde Park. It had an elaborate entrance, with hanging gardens providing a multicolored screen for the smoke-tinted glass of the lobby.

Thinking that there was a possibility that Ular was watching, Carol turned the car into the underground parking entrance, ignoring the stern signs that announced that it was for tenants *only*. She stopped the car in a slot marked for service vehicles. Bourke took the black armband from his sleeve and got out of the car.

Ferguson had been watching for them. He hurried up to the car, saying, "No sign of Ular. I'll take you to the building supervisor. Julia Pell is with him. I caught her just before she got in the lift for the penthouse."

Before Ferguson opened an unobtrusive unmarked door near the security desk in the lobby, he said, "Name of Featherstone. He's a Pom."

Featherstone was very British. He had a rigidly upright stance and a clipped toothbrush mustache. His receding black hair — Carol thought that, along with his mustache, it might be dyed — was brushed straight back so it formed a thin dark cap over his skull. He wore a tweed jacket and brown knife-creased trousers, and his tan shoes were polished to mirror perfection.

"How'd you do?" he said in a marbles-in-mouth accent. It was a pragmatic courtesy. He was obviously unhappy to have the police within the precincts of his building.

A spindly woman sitting in the corner of Featherstone's office leaped to her feet as soon as they came in. "Julia Pell," she announced before Featherstone could introduce her. "I've been waiting for you for ages. Your man won't let me go up."

Shaking hands with Carol, and then Bourke, she went on in her high, piping voice, "I mean, it's just too bad, isn't it, that Granger should have to worry about something like this. The man must be a maniac, a positive maniac. Deranged, even, don't you think?"

She was one of those people of indeterminate age, who probably had looked very much the same all her life. She had light brown hair, strangely textured like beige cotton wool, and a mobile face that changed expression constantly.

She dug into her voluminous tapestry handbag. "We're going up to the penthouse now?"

"We would like to check the apartment before you enter it," said Carol.

Julia looked at her sharply. "Check for what? You think there's a bomb up there? I was in the other day, and it was perfectly all right. I must say, Granger keeps everything very neat, unlike other men I've known. My second ex-husband for one. Positive pig of a man."

Featherstone insisted that he should accompany Bourke and Ferguson. "I am responsible for the building," he said, as though that were reason enough to join in police business.

He went on, "Justice Granger Flint has one of

179

our two penthouses, and I feel secure in claiming that they are equal to any luxury apartment in the city of Sydney. They have, naturally, million-dollar views. Balconies, every facility for gracious living —"

"Thank you, Mr. Featherstone." Carol cut him off before he could launch into a more detailed description of the prime qualities of the building. "I must ask that you stay outside the apartment until we are sure that it is safe."

"Harrumph! We have state-of-the-art security."

"Ray Unwin, the handyman you hired — did he have access to all parts of the building?"

Featherstone threw back his head and looked down his nose at Carol. "Only those areas where it was necessary for him to be."

Bourke said, "Did that include inside the apartments?"

"Well, of course. Unwin was responsible for minor plumbing, sticking window catches, that sort of thing."

"And if no one was home, how did he get in?"

A slight flush colored Featherstone's cheeks. "A master key . . ." He rallied to add, "But he handed it back to me as soon as the job was done."

While the three men went up to the penthouse, Carol sat down with Julia Pell. "I'm sorry for this inconvenience, but we are concerned about your brother-in-law's safety."

Julia's wide mouth turned down at the corners. "I know all about the Reginald Ular trial," she declared. "Hideous man. Hideous."

"This is the suspect." Carol handed her a photograph.

Her eyebrows shot up. "Oh, yes. This photo was

in the newspaper. I can't say he looks familiar, though, you know, I must have seen him many times. He's got one of those humdrum faces, once seen, always forgotten." She chuckled at her remark. "Not bad, eh? Once seen, always forgotten?"

"Not bad," said Carol. "Where did you see him?"

"Well, not recently, Inspector, worse luck for you. I mean at his brother's trial. He was there every day, I remember, sitting with the parents."

She pursed her lips. "Brutal look about the father, I thought. Wouldn't be a bit surprised if he were a pervert, too. And the mother was a washed-out looking thing. Spineless, I shouldn't be surprised."

Intrigued, Carol said, "Were you there for the verdict?"

"Of course I was. Wouldn't miss it. And the sentencing, too, of course." Julia's face was split by a huge grin. "Bit of a trial junkie, I am. My last husband always complained I spent too much time in courtrooms. I told him it was my hobby, but he still whined about it nonstop. And it wasn't as if *he* had any interests. Boring man. Can't imagine why I married him."

Carol blinked. Julia became reflective. "Had four," she said. "Husbands, that is. Sworn off them now. Too much trouble."

Amused, Carol had to resist the temptation to go off in pursuit of Julia Pell's marital tribulations. "You were there for the Ular verdict, you said?"

"It was cut and dried. The confession to the cops, if nothing else, sealed his fate. Reg Ular just stood there, stony faced, while the verdict was read. I recall I looked at the family — the father, mainly, because I wanted to see how he took it. I wouldn't have been

181

surprised if he'd started a scene, shouted, and threatened. That sort of man can turn nasty very easily, I've found. But he didn't do anything. The son was the one — Philip. He just broke down and sobbed. You could hear him through the whole courtroom. Put his hands over his face and cried his heart out."

Her face twisted in distaste. "Brotherly love, I suppose, but imagine crying over a monster like that."

Bourke came through the door, followed by Featherstone. "The penthouse is clear," Bourke said. "I've left Ferguson on guard. We'll keep someone there until the judge is back."

"Excellent idea," said Julia, bounding to her feet. "I hope he or she won't mind watering the plants and doing a final tidy before Granger gets home. He's very particular. One time he was away, I lost his favorite fern. Don't know what I did, but it gave up the ghost and wilted all over the place. Granger gave me hell, I can tell you."

Repressing a laugh, Carol suggested that she might like to check the mail. Julia led the way out the door to the lifts. "Right, and we're looking for a chain letter. I've got that clear," she said over her shoulder.

The penthouse was beautiful. Graceful furniture, thick white carpeting, feathery ferns in porcelain containers.

"Antiques, every one of them," said Julia, tapping her fingernails against a glowing yellow urn near the door.

Ferguson stood near a black marble stand on

which was heaped a tidy pile of envelopes. "I've had a quick look. I think this is it," he said.

The envelope was similar to the one found in Janet McGary's rubbish bin, white with the name and address printed in block capitals.

"Do you mind if we open it?" asked Bourke.

Julia was staring at the envelope with fascination. "I didn't even notice it. Looks nothing like a bill, that's why."

Bourke slit the envelope with a penknife and slid the single page out, unfolding it carefully so that he touched only the edges of the paper. "There it is," he said.

The body of the letter was identical to the one Ferguson had found in Orbe's shed, but the quotation was different.

Wherein thou judgest another, thou condemnest thyself.

Maureen Oatland regarded the photograph of Granger Flint supplied by Julia Pell. "Not much of a looker, is he? Certainly not my type. My old man's got nothing to worry about."

"Be on your best behavior," said Carol, her lips twitching. The thought of Maureen playing the role of a new romantic interest in Judge Flint's life was irresistibly amusing.

"Okay, Maureen," said Bourke. "Let's get this straight. You go out on the pilot's launch to meet the judge's ship as it comes through the Heads."

"I throw up if it gets rough," said Maureen.

Bourke ignored that. "Justice Flint's been alerted as to what's happening, and he'll be waiting for you in the captain's quarters, where you'll give him a detailed briefing about what to do. When you leave the ship, it'll be on his arm. As far as anyone on the dock is concerned, you are his shipboard romance."

"Fuck a duck! A judge!" Maureen gave a neigh of laughter. "I'll have to put on my best duds!"

CHAPTER SIXTEEN

The alarm gave a muted shriek. Carol swung a hand to slap it off, then stretched and yawned. The clear dawn light indicated that the rain had gone for good. She listened but couldn't hear Sybil moving about.

Last night they'd met for dinner at a local Italian restaurant. It wasn't Carol's favorite cuisine, but Sybil had a weakness for pasta, any pasta, and Carol was determined to indulge her in any way possible.

Over the meal Carol had renewed her objections to Sybil going back to her own house. "You have no idea how much it worries me that you're there alone," she had said to Sybil. "I can't give you any of the details, but I think we have a good chance of catching him tomorrow, and then you'll be safe. It's tonight I'm concerned about."

Sybil had paused with a forkful of spaghetti half-way to her mouth. "Is this a ploy to get me into bed?"

Although her tone was light, Carol felt a warning flicker of caution. Sybil was skittish, still doubtful of where — if anywhere — their relationship was going.

"Not a ploy," Carol said, "although it's a delightful thought. I was going to suggest the guest bedroom." She leaned across the table and put her hand over Sybil's. "Please. Philip Ular is a psycho-path. If he has the motivation, he's capable of any-thing. And you've given it to him, just by doing your duty all those years ago."

Sybil nodded slowly. "Okay, you've persuaded me. Just for tonight, and the guest bedroom."

When they'd arrived home, Carol had been scrupulously careful to treat Sybil like a dear friend, not a lover. They'd had a drink, watched some tele-vision, then gone to their separate rooms.

Carol had been awake for a long time, but the only movement in the house had not been Sybil coming in to join her, but a short spat between Sinker and Jeffrey about who was going to claim the foot of Carol's bed. Sinker won, and Jeffrey had stalked off, presumably to sleep with Sybil.

Carol quietly dressed in her running gear and

walked softly down the hallway to the other bedroom. Sybil was still asleep, curled up with the sheet pulled up so that all Carol could see was her red hair.

Her heart turned over. What she felt was so much more complex than what before she had called love.

When Carol came back from her run, Sybil was dressed and sitting at the kitchen bench with a cup of tea and the morning paper. "Look at this," she said, pointing to a headline on the third page. She read it aloud with suitable emphasis. "Juror Terror. Widow asks: Was a maniac stalking me?"

"I hope juror terror can die down after today," Carol said dryly.

"Can you tell me anything about what's happening?" Giving Carol a beguiling smile, she added, "After all, I have a vested interest, since you keep assuring me I'm high on Philip Ular's list."

"All I can say is that someone's coming back into the country who definitely figures on his hit list, and that he may attempt to kill him, possibly today."

"So you've set a trap?"

"Yes. And if he takes the bait, we've got him."

While showering, Carol ran through key points in the day ahead. Granger Flint's cruise ship would dock at three that afternoon, and everything had to be firmly in place before then. Bourke had had the task of finding a suitable double for the judge, and when she had left work yesterday he had it down to three possibilities.

Since Monday, either Ferguson or Brooks had been resident in the judge's penthouse, and other officers would take their positions in the building after the briefing she and Mark would give at nine this morning.

No one whom Ular might recognize could be in any public area near the apartments, so that precluded both Mark and herself, as well as anyone else who had been at any of the crime scenes.

Carol had undertaken to attend Janet McGary's funeral that morning at eleven-thirty, so she had decided to leave Mark Bourke in control of the operation, which he had code-named Operation Guppy. "Guppies are little fish," he'd explained. "I'm thinking a little fish to catch a big one."

Carol had laughed and said that she thought the bait they were using, namely Justice Flint, would object to being called a little fish, since he'd spent most of his legal life being an extremely large one.

As she toweled herself dry, she reviewed the steps of the operation. Were there any holes in the net? Weak places that Philip Ular, if he took the bait, might break through?

"You're wearing black?" said Sybil when Carol came out to collect her things.

"I'm going to Janet McGary's funeral this afternoon. I was going to simply choose something dark, but somehow, since I wore black to Steve York's service, I feel I have to do the same for her."

"You surprise me, Carol, sometimes."

"I do?"

"You do." She gave Carol a light kiss on the cheek. "Have a good day. Before I leave I'll lock up and make sure the cats won't starve."

"And tonight?" said Carol casually.

"Tonight? Call me at home and tell me what's happened. We can take it from there."

As Carol unlocked her car, Jenny, wearing her paint-stained smock, came out to the street. "I'm getting a quote on the fence that's falling down between us. Can I send the guy in to look at it from your side?"

An alarm automatically sounded in Carol's mind. "Who is he?"

"The fencer? Dave's Fencing, he calls himself. He's been working in the area for years. Did Mae's brush fence on the corner. Nice job, I thought."

"Sure, he can come in." Carol glanced at her watch. "Hell, I've got to go."

When she arrived at work, Bourke was waiting for her. "It's been bloody hard to come up with a convincing double for the judge," said Bourke, "but I think I've done it. Height and build are about the same." He flashed a Polaroid photo at Carol. "Well, what do you think? It's Cec Swallow from fraud."

Carol compared the two photographs. The image of the real Granger Flint showed a fat slab of a face with a complacent half smile on his full lips. The few remaining strands of his hair were combed carefully to cover his skull. His heavy eyebrows were still dark and gave an emphatic stamp to the top half of his face.

The decoy Bourke had selected had insignificant eyebrows, but he was satisfactorily bald and had the same general shape to the thick block of his face. "Not bad. Not bad at all."

"The eyebrows will be fixed, of course, and we have a full description of what Flint will be wearing when he leaves the ship, so it should work, especially as Ular will only see him from a distance."

In the briefing room, Carol spoke first. "I need hardly remind you that Philip Ular is extremely dangerous. He's a multiple murderer and won't hesitate to kill again. If you do see him, don't be fooled by his mild manner. He'll be armed and will use lethal force to escape arrest."

Bourke took over. "Maureen will be on the ship when it docks at three o'clock this afternoon at the Overseas Terminal. She'll disembark with the judge, and they'll be under surveillance continuously from that moment on."

He gestured to Maureen Oatland, who was lounging on a chair near the front. "Okay, Maureen, tell it from your side."

Beaming, Maureen got to her feet. "Well, Justice Flint and I — of course, I'll be calling him Granger — come off the boat with eyes only for each other. Because he's a judge, we get special treatment, so we don't have to worry about the luggage in the hold, but we go straight to a special custom's area for VIPs. It's a private room, and that's where the switch is made."

She gave a derisive snort. "And it's there I lose a judge and gain Cec Swallow!"

The laughter that greeted this sally, Carol knew, had a lot to do with release of tension.

Maureen continued, "Justice Flint stays with an armed guard, and Cec and I are ushered into a waiting stretch limo for the trip to the judge's penthouse." She grinned at Mills. "And Bryant here will be the limo driver, but he's got a slim chance of getting a tip, I can tell you."

Bourke broke in, "The limousine has heavily tinted windows, so Ular can't get a good look at them. We'll have two cars, one following, one a half block in front. You know the route, Bryant, and we've arranged with traffic control to switch the lights to green at each intersection as you approach. If something happens, such as the deliberate blocking of the limo, don't be a hero, but get out of there any way you can. The officers shadowing you can move in and arrest Ular. The limo will be equipped with a siren, and there'll be a portable red light ready to slap on the roof. Jump the median strip, if necessary, and do a U-turn."

"Right," said Mills, clearly delighted with his part in the operation. Carol suspected he almost hoped something would go wrong so he could use the evasive driving techniques he'd been taught at the police driving school.

"If the transfer from the ship goes smoothly, as we expect it will," said Bourke, "it means that Ular will make his attack once the target is in the building. This is how it's set up: Ferguson is already in the judge's penthouse; Brooks will be on standby in the penthouse next door; Standish is the new handyman, and he'll stay close to Featherstone, the building supervisor; and when the limo arrives, Richards will be in the lobby, posing as a visitor to one of the other apartments."

Richards spoke up around the wad of gum he constantly chewed. "What's to stop Ular from driving into the parking area with a car bomb?"

"You'll be happy to know we've thought of that. Fletcher from the bomb squad — we couldn't use Ned Cromwell because he was at the McGary crime scene

—will park an electrician's van in the basement and then vet the building, from the roof down. Fletcher will have an electrician's apprentice with him, and since he had to look like a callow youth, we decided Miles would fit the bill."

There was general laughter at this, and the subject of the attention blushed. Constable Miles Li looked so young that he was frequently embarrassed by demands for proof of age when he tried to have a drink after work with his colleagues.

Carol was satisfied that Operation Guppy was under control. The financier who owned the neighboring penthouse had been very helpful, agreeing to move out at a day's notice. Featherstone, clearly appalled at what was happening in his beloved structure, was cooperating, but with a pained expression that showed the cost to his peace of mind.

"Back to you, Maureen," said Bourke.

She was more than willing to retake center stage. "When the limo stops in front of the building, Cec Swallow, playing the judge, tenderly helps me out, and we walk into the lobby, fast, so there's not much time to get a good look at him. Bryant follows us with the hand luggage we have, puts the bags down, and, after making sure Alec Richards is in place, he leaves. Alec presses the button for a floor about halfway up, but when we stop on that floor, he doesn't get out. When the three of us reach the top, Alec goes up on the roof of the building and waits there, while Cec and I enter the penthouse, where, frankly, I intend to have a stiff whiskey to tide me over."

Carol checked her watch. "Janet McGary's funeral

starts in forty minutes," she said to Bourke. "I'd better go. Contact me if anything urgent happens."

Even in the bright sunlight, the gray walls of St. Luke's were dignified and solemn. It seemed the whole congregation had turned out for Janet's funeral. The dark pews were packed with people, some in casual clothes, others obviously dressed in their best. The casket of light oak had a spray of red and white roses, whose vibrancy made the ceremony more poignant.

The choir sang, not beautifully, but with feeling. Carol didn't know enough to detect if the alto line was weakened by Janet's absence, but she did note the frantic straining of the sopranos and the flushed faces of the tenors. The psalms and hymns were affecting, and Reverend Mette spoke eloquently about Janet McGary's sterling role in St. Luke's parish family.

Carol was not surprised to find that Nordica Anderson-Mette was not present at the service. She scanned the pews covertly for Philip Ular, but didn't really expect to see him, as he had the judge's return to occupy his attention.

It was a bleak replay of Steve's funeral, except that the sun was shining. After the service, Carol found herself mouthing the same platitudes to Alice McGary that she had used with Lauren and Steve's parents. There was nothing original to say. It was simply that someone was dead, and the world was poorer for it.

She watched the casket loaded into the sleek hearse, and suddenly knew, urgently, that she must tell Sybil the depth of her feelings. How trite to say that life was fleeting, eternity long. She knew these thoughts weren't original, but now, for some reason, she felt their weight.

Back in the car, she called Sybil at school, hoping to get her between lessons. "She's not here today," said the woman who answered.

"But she must be."

"Sorry. She reported in sick."

Frowning, Carol snapped the cell phone shut. Sybil was conscientious, almost too conscientious. It was so unlike her to call in and say she was ill, when she wasn't.

She punched in Sybil's home number. The phone rang four times, then Sybil's recorded voice picked up. Carol didn't leave a message.

Wondering if perhaps Jeffrey had taken a turn for the worse, she checked with the veterinary clinic, but he hadn't been taken back there for treatment.

Next she called the office, but Bourke had already left to set up the command post in an unmarked car a kilometer from the apartments.

"Inspector, Anne Newsome wants to speak with you."

"Put her on."

Anne's voice was triumphant. "I told you she'd call."

"Who?"

"Justine Ular. Her husband's out, and she called me."

"Anything of interest?"

"She wouldn't tell me. She wants to talk with you. Says it's important." Anne couldn't hide the chagrin in her voice.

Carol sighed. "Give me her number."

She debated whether to call. She was puzzled — no, worried — about Sybil. She punched in the number of Sybil's local police station and identified herself, asking them to send a patrol car to check if Sybil's car was there and to see if anyone was in the house. "I'll call back in half an hour."

She looked at Justine Ular's number, and debated whether to call. Justine answered on the first ring, her voice breathy and anxious. "Hello?"

"This is Inspector Carol Ashton. We met on Saturday. You wanted to speak with me?"

"I can't talk for long. Malcolm's out, you see, but he'll be back soon."

"How can I help you?"

"I saw it was that poor teacher's funeral today, the one that was blown up, and that made me think of that other teacher . . . I heard them talking, you know. That red-haired bitch, Malcolm said — forgive the language, but it's what he said."

Carol was chilled. She looked through the windscreen and saw the hearse pull away, bearing Janet McGary's body to the Northern Suburbs Crematorium. "Was Malcolm talking to Philip when you overheard him?"

"I'm sure he was. I couldn't tell you before, but I know it's so wrong what Reg did, and now, what Philip is doing . . ." Her voice faded, as though she were moving away from the phone.

"Are you there?" Carol could hear the urgent fear in her own voice. "Justine?"

"If it hadn't been for her, Reg would be alive today . . . That's what Malcolm said. And Philip, I know he agreed. He always had this special relationship with his father."

195

"When was this conversation?"

In the background there was a flat sound. A front door slamming? "Malcolm's back," Justine whispered. "He mustn't catch me talking to you." The connection was broken.

Carol looked at her watch. There was plenty of time before the judge's ship docked. She called Anne back and told her that she would be back in the office in ninety minutes.

Confident that Bourke could run Operation Guppy without her, and driven by an urgency she couldn't explain, Carol drove home. The Harbour Bridge, Military Road, the S-bends, the bridge at the Spit — all flowed easily, without problems. She even caught mostly green traffic lights.

It felt strange to be driving these familiar roads so early on a Wednesday. She turned into her own street and saw that Sybil's car wasn't in the carport. How stupid to have driven home, for nothing. Sybil had probably decided to skip work and go shopping.

No, she knew that wasn't a possibility. Perhaps the person who had answered the phone at the school was mistaken, and Sybil *was* there . . .

She parked. Got out of the car. Touched the butt of the little Glock in its holster in the small of her back. It was palm-size, but deadly. She knew its dimensions and weight: 160 millimeters by 106 millimeters, and 560 grams in weight. Nine rounds and one in the chamber. Ten in total.

She knew that Philip Ular was stalking Granger Flint, that right now he was kilometers away, waiting for his next victim to step on shore from the safety of a cruise ship. She took a deep breath. She'd just check the house, see if Jeffrey was still okay. And

Sybil might have decided to do something unexpected. Maybe she'd left a note.

The house was quiet, passive. The birds were silent, and the buzz of bees in the flowers seemed very loud. She saw a flash of blue — a little wren, building a nest in a garden bush. She had to make sure that the cats didn't decide to help themselves to the fledglings, when they hatched.

Carol moved toward the house. It looked as it always did, a building well-qualified to sit among the gumtrees as an integral part of the landscape. She took out her key, and opened the front door.

A sound . . . a moan? . . . drifted down the hall.

"Sybil?"

She took out her gun.

"Come in," said a light male voice. "You're in time to see her die."

CHAPTER SEVENTEEN

"I believe this might be called a stalemate." His tone was pleasantly conversational.

Carol stood at the entrance to the sitting room, balanced on the balls of her feet. She held the Glock 27 automatic in both extended hands, its black wickedness almost hidden by her fingers.

Philip Ular, a half smile on his face, leaned back against the breakfast bar. He wore faded jeans and a white T-shirt with the words DAVE'S FENCING and an illustration of a paling fence. His weapon, a silver large-frame revolver, was considerably more substantial than her subcompact Glock.

At last the monster she had been pursuing had taken on a physical reality. In the studio photograph, taken by a professional for an acting portfolio, clever lighting had made Philip Ular's features more significant than they were in actuality. His face was ordinary, banal. There was nothing individual or striking about him. Mundane evil.

She expected him to be disguised in some way, perhaps with a mustache or dyed hair. He hadn't bothered.

"What is that?" he said. "It looks like a toy gun."

"It isn't."

She took a step forward. Out of the corner of her eye Carol could see Sybil's body slumped on the brightly-patterned mat in front of the couch. The handcuffs on her wrists caught the light. Her head was turned away, so Carol couldn't see her face.

"This" — Ular gestured fractionally with the thick barrel — "is a forty-five. Smith and Wesson. Cost me an arm and a leg on the black market. I got it on the Gold Coast." He grinned. "So many good things come from Queensland."

He cocked his head. "I watched you leave this morning in such a hurry, so you can imagine how surprised I am to see you here now, since I would have thought that you'd be fully occupied with Justice Flint." He clicked his tongue in mock annoyance. "And after I'd gone to all the trouble to move her car to another street so that Jenny next door wouldn't be tempted to pay a social call, I expected not to be interrupted by anyone."

199

Sybil groaned, and a shudder ran through her body. Carol took another step to put herself in a position so that she could see Sybil more clearly.

The barrel of the big gun followed her unerringly. "I suppose you think it unsporting that I didn't send a chain letter this time. I did have an excellent quote picked out — something about Jezebel being eaten by dogs — but under the circumstances it did seem self-defeating to warn her, since I had the judge set up to keep you occupied."

Sybil's breathing seemed more labored. Carol took another step.

"Have a good look," he said. "She may regain consciousness for a moment or two. She'll put a good show on, if she does. She was having some quite spectacular hallucinations before she passed out."

Keeping the Glock aligned on him, Carol risked another quick glance. Now Sybil had turned her head, and Carol could see that her nose and mouth were bruised and bleeding. Her breathing was rough, loud in the sunny room.

"She fought taking her medicine," he said.

Carol had to know what Sybil had been given. "Her medicine?"

"Gammahydroxybutyrate," he said, pronouncing each syllable with care. "You cops know it as Fantasy."

Carol knew it well. A designer party drug, Fantasy was also known as GHB, or by humorists, GBH, which stood for grievous bodily harm.

"How much did you give her?"

He shrugged, the action hardly moving the gun centered on Carol's body. "It was the liquid form. I just held her nose and poured it into her mouth. It took a while, because she wouldn't cooperate. I don't know how much she got, but I'm sure its a fatal dose. That's the most important thing."

Carol's heart was hammering so hard she thought he must hear it. As with all designer drugs, Fantasy had complex side effects that varied from person to person, but an overdose of GHB almost always led to altered states of consciousness, followed by coma and respiratory failure.

"Get out of here," she said. "You can't shoot me without having me return the fire. Just walk out, backward. I won't follow you."

He shook his head. "It doesn't work that way. Put down that toy gun and maybe I'll let you call an ambulance. She might be saved, if she gets medical attention straightaway."

His tone was reasonable, his expression helpful.

Carol said, "Red-haired bitch, that's what your father called her, isn't it? Do you really want her to live after what she did to your brother?"

His inoffensive, ordinary face was swept with ferocious rage. "The bitch has to die!"

"Die? I don't think so. She seems to be doing okay to me."

Involuntarily, Philip Ular looked toward Sybil's body. The barrel of the heavy revolver wavered for a moment.

Carol fired once, twice, three times.

The gun in his hand discharged, the bullet plowing into the wall near her head. His next round went into the polished floor, as his knees buckled.

He looked at the spreading red stain on his shirt, then, with terrible effort, raised the forty-five, aiming it not at Carol, but at Sybil. "Bitch!" he screamed.

Carol fired again. He jerked, and slid down the breakfast bar to sit on the floor. Carol leapt toward him, sent his revolver spinning away across the room.

He looked up at her. "You haven't killed me," he said. "I can't die until every one of them has been punished."

CHAPTER EIGHTEEN

"He's critically injured," said Carol, "but Philip Ular will live to go to trial."

Sybil looked up from the couch where she was lying. She had spent two days in hospital and then Carol had brought her back to the house at the beach.

"Pity," Sybil said thickly through swollen lips.

"Yes."

Outside the open doors of Sybil's living room, the ocean, sky, and land collaborated to create their usual magic. A lone cockatoo hung in the air, shrieking, then spun in a lazy arc and disappeared from view.

Carol took Sybil's hand, examining the fingers, the palm. "If only I —"

"Don't start on a guilt trip, Carol." Sybil's bruised mouth stretched in an attempt at a smile. "You *were* going to, weren't you?"

"When Jenny mentioned Dave's Fencing and said he'd been working in the area for years, I just assumed she knew him herself. But she didn't. It was just what Philip Ular had told her, and she took it at face value." Carol pressed her lips together. "That was stupid and careless of me."

"Will anything I say make a difference?"

"No."

Sounding amused, Sybil said, "Then I won't say anything." Her face changed, as she went on, "Carol, I don't think I can go back to that house. Not yet, anyway. What happened was . . ." She put a hand across her mouth as her eyes filled with tears. "Sorry."

"That's quite okay. This afternoon I'm collecting Jeffrey and Sinker and we're moving down here."

"You are?"

"You desperately need a bodyguard," said Carol. "And frankly, I'm it."

A few of the publications of
THE NAIAD PRESS, INC.
P.O. Box 10543 • Tallahassee, Florida 32302
Phone (850) 539-5965
Toll-Free Order Number: 1-800-533-1973
Mail orders welcome. Please include 15% postage.
Write or call for our free catalog which also features an
incredible selection of lesbian videos.

LADY BE GOOD edited by Barbara Grier and Christine Cassidy. Erotic stories by Naiad Press authors. 288 pp. ISBN 1-56280-180-5 $14.95

CHAIN LETTER by Claire McNab. 288 pp. 9th Carol Ashton mystery.   ISBN 1-56280-181-3   11.95

NIGHT VISION by Laura Adams. 256 pp. Erotic fantasy romance by "famous" author.   ISBN 1-56280-182-1   11.95

SEA TO SHINING SEA by Lisa Shapiro. 256 pp. Unable to resist the raging passion . . .   ISBN 1-56280-177-5   11.95

THIRD DEGREE by Kate Calloway. 224 pp. 3rd Cassidy James mystery.   ISBN 1-56280-185-6   11.95

WHEN THE DANCING STOPS by Therese Szymanski. 272 pp. 1st Brett Higgins mystery.   ISBN 1-56280-186-4   11.95

PHASES OF THE MOON by Julia Watts. 192 pp. . . . . hungry for everything life has to offer.   ISBN 1-56280-176-7   11.95

BABY IT'S COLD by Jaye Maiman. 256 pp. 5th Robin Miller mystery.   ISBN 1-56280-156-2   10.95

CLASS REUNION by Linda Hill. 176 pp. The girl from her past . . .   ISBN 1-56280-178-3   11.95

DREAM LOVER by Lyn Denison. 224 pp. A soft, sensuous, romantic fantasy.   ISBN 1-56280-173-1   11.95

FORTY LOVE by Diana Simmonds. 288 pp. Joyous, heart-warming romance.   ISBN 1-56280-171-6   11.95

IN THE MOOD by Robbi Sommers. 160 pp. The queen of erotic tension!   ISBN 1-56280-172-4   11.95

SWIMMING CAT COVE by Lauren Douglas. 192 pp. 2nd Allison O'Neil Mystery.   ISBN 1-56280-168-6   11.95

THE LOVING LESBIAN by Claire McNab and Sharon Gedan. 240 pp. Explore the experiences that make lesbian love unique.   ISBN 1-56280-169-4   14.95

COURTED by Celia Cohen. 160 pp. Sparkling romantic
encounter.   ISBN 1-56280-166-X   11.95

SEASONS OF THE HEART by Jackie Calhoun. 240 pp. Romance
through the years.   ISBN 1-56280-167-8   11.95

K. C. BOMBER by Janet McClellan. 208 pp. 1st Tru North
mystery.   ISBN 1-56280-157-0   11.95

LAST RITES by Tracey Richardson. 192 pp. 1st Stevie Houston
mystery.   ISBN 1-56280-164-3   11.95

EMBRACE IN MOTION by Karin Kallmaker. 256 pp. A whirlwind
love affair.   ISBN 1-56280-165-1   11.95

HOT CHECK by Peggy J. Herring. 192 pp. Will workaholic Alice
fall for guitarist Ricky?   ISBN 1-56280-163-5   11.95

OLD TIES by Saxon Bennett. 176 pp. Can Cleo surrender to a
passionate new love?   ISBN 1-56280-159-7   11.95

LOVE ON THE LINE by Laura DeHart Young. 176 pp. Will Stef
win Kay's heart?   ISBN 1-56280-162-7   11.95

DEVIL'S LEG CROSSING by Kaye Davis. 192 pp. 1st Maris Middleton
mystery.   ISBN 1-56280-158-9   11.95

COSTA BRAVA by Marta Balletbo Coll. 144 pp. Read the book,
see the movie!   ISBN 1-56280-153-8   11.95

MEETING MAGDALENE & OTHER STORIES by
Marilyn Freeman. 144 pp. Read the book, see the movie!
                                               ISBN 1-56280-170-8   11.95

SECOND FIDDLE by Kate Calloway. 208 pp. P.I. Cassidy James'
second case.   ISBN 1-56280-169-6   11.95

LAUREL by Isabel Miller. 128 pp. By the author of the beloved
Patience and Sarah.   ISBN 1-56280-146-5   10.95

LOVE OR MONEY by Jackie Calhoun. 240 pp. The romance of
real life.   ISBN 1-56280-147-3   10.95

SMOKE AND MIRRORS by Pat Welch. 224 pp. 5th Helen Black
Mystery.   ISBN 1-56280-143-0   10.95

DANCING IN THE DARK edited by Barbara Grier & Christine
Cassidy. 272 pp. Erotic love stories by Naiad Press authors.
                                               ISBN 1-56280-144-9   14.95

TIME AND TIME AGAIN by Catherine Ennis. 176 pp. Passionate
love affair.   ISBN 1-56280-145-7   10.95

PAXTON COURT by Diane Salvatore. 256 pp. Erotic and wickedly
funny contemporary tale about the business of learning to live
together.   ISBN 1-56280-114-7   10.95

INNER CIRCLE by Claire McNab. 208 pp. 8th Carol Ashton
Mystery.   ISBN 1-56280-135-X   11.95

LESBIAN SEX: AN ORAL HISTORY by Susan Johnson.
240 pp. Need we say more? ISBN 1-56280-142-2   14.95

WILD THINGS by Karin Kallmaker. 240 pp. By the undisputed
mistress of lesbian romance. ISBN 1-56280-139-2   11.95

THE GIRL NEXT DOOR by Mindy Kaplan. 208 pp. Just what
you'd expect. ISBN 1-56280-140-6   11.95

NOW AND THEN by Penny Hayes. 240 pp. Romance on the
westward journey. ISBN 1-56280-121-X   11.95

HEART ON FIRE by Diana Simmonds. 176 pp. The romantic and
erotic rival of *Curious Wine.* ISBN 1-56280-152-X   11.95

DEATH AT LAVENDER BAY by Lauren Wright Douglas. 208 pp.
1st Allison O'Neil Mystery. ISBN 1-56280-085-X   11.95

YES I SAID YES I WILL by Judith McDaniel. 272 pp. Hot
romance by famous author. ISBN 1-56280-138-4   11.95

FORBIDDEN FIRES by Margaret C. Anderson. Edited by Mathilda
Hills. 176 pp. Famous author's "unpublished" Lesbian romance.
ISBN 1-56280-123-6   21.95

SIDE TRACKS by Teresa Stores. 160 pp. Gender-bending
Lesbians on the road. ISBN 1-56280-122-8   10.95

HOODED MURDER by Annette Van Dyke. 176 pp. 1st Jessie
Batelle Mystery. ISBN 1-56280-134-1   10.95

WILDWOOD FLOWERS by Julia Watts. 208 pp. Hilarious and
heart-warming tale of true love. ISBN 1-56280-127-9   10.95

NEVER SAY NEVER by Linda Hill. 224 pp. Rule #1: Never get involved
with . . . ISBN 1-56280-126-0   10.95

THE SEARCH by Melanie McAllester. 240 pp. Exciting top cop
Tenny Mendoza case. ISBN 1-56280-150-3   10.95

THE WISH LIST by Saxon Bennett. 192 pp. Romance through
the years. ISBN 1-56280-125-2   10.95

FIRST IMPRESSIONS by Kate Calloway. 208 pp. P.I. Cassidy
James' first case. ISBN 1-56280-133-3   10.95

OUT OF THE NIGHT by Kris Bruyer. 192 pp. Spine-tingling
thriller. ISBN 1-56280-120-1   10.95

NORTHERN BLUE by Tracey Richardson. 224 pp. Police recruits
Miki & Miranda — passion in the line of fire. ISBN 1-56280-118-X   10.95

LOVE'S HARVEST by Peggy J. Herring. 176 pp. by the author of
Once More With Feeling. ISBN 1-56280-117-1   10.95

THE COLOR OF WINTER by Lisa Shapiro. 208 pp. Romantic
love beyond your wildest dreams. ISBN 1-56280-116-3   10.95

FAMILY SECRETS by Laura DeHart Young. 208 pp. Enthralling
romance and suspense. ISBN 1-56280-119-8   10.95

INLAND PASSAGE by Jane Rule. 288 pp. Tales exploring conventional & unconventional relationships.   ISBN 0-930044-56-8   10.95

DOUBLE BLUFF by Claire McNab. 208 pp. 7th Carol Ashton Mystery.   ISBN 1-56280-096-5   10.95

BAR GIRLS by Lauran Hoffman. 176 pp. See the movie, read the book!   ISBN 1-56280-115-5   10.95

THE FIRST TIME EVER edited by Barbara Grier & Christine Cassidy. 272 pp. Love stories by Naiad Press authors.
                                                        ISBN 1-56280-086-8   14.95

MISS PETTIBONE AND MISS McGRAW by Brenda Weathers. 208 pp. A charming ghostly love story.   ISBN 1-56280-151-1   10.95

CHANGES by Jackie Calhoun. 208 pp. Involved romance and relationships.   ISBN 1-56280-083-3   10.95

FAIR PLAY by Rose Beecham. 256 pp. 3rd Amanda Valentine Mystery.   ISBN 1-56280-081-7   10.95

PAYBACK by Celia Cohen. 176 pp. A gripping thriller of romance, revenge and betrayal.   ISBN 1-56280-084-1   10.95

THE BEACH AFFAIR by Barbara Johnson. 224 pp. Sizzling summer romance/mystery/intrigue.   ISBN 1-56280-090-6   10.95

GETTING THERE by Robbi Sommers. 192 pp. Nobody does it like Robbi!   ISBN 1-56280-099-X   10.95

FINAL CUT by Lisa Haddock. 208 pp. 2nd Carmen Ramirez Mystery.   ISBN 1-56280-088-4   10.95

FLASHPOINT by Katherine V. Forrest. 256 pp. A Lesbian blockbuster!   ISBN 1-56280-079-5   10.95

CLAIRE OF THE MOON by Nicole Conn. Audio Book —Read by Marianne Hyatt.   ISBN 1-56280-113-9   16.95

FOR LOVE AND FOR LIFE: INTIMATE PORTRAITS OF LESBIAN COUPLES by Susan Johnson. 224 pp.
                                                        ISBN 1-56280-091-4   14.95

DEVOTION by Mindy Kaplan. 192 pp. See the movie — read the book!   ISBN 1-56280-093-0   10.95

SOMEONE TO WATCH by Jaye Maiman. 272 pp. 4th Robin Miller Mystery.   ISBN 1-56280-095-7   10.95

GREENER THAN GRASS by Jennifer Fulton. 208 pp. A young woman — a stranger in her bed.   ISBN 1-56280-092-2   10.95

TRAVELS WITH DIANA HUNTER by Regine Sands. Erotic lesbian romp. Audio Book (2 cassettes)   ISBN 1-56280-107-4   16.95

CABIN FEVER by Carol Schmidt. 256 pp. Sizzling suspense and passion.   ISBN 1-56280-089-1   10.95

THERE WILL BE NO GOODBYES by Laura DeHart Young. 192 pp. Romantic love, strength, and friendship.   ISBN 1-56280-103-1   10.95

FAULTLINE by Sheila Ortiz Taylor. 144 pp. Joyous comic
lesbian novel.   ISBN 1-56280-108-2   9.95

OPEN HOUSE by Pat Welch. 176 pp. 4th Helen Black Mystery.
                                                        ISBN 1-56280-102-3   10.95

ONCE MORE WITH FEELING by Peggy J. Herring. 240 pp.
Lighthearted, loving romantic adventure.   ISBN 1-56280-089-2   10.95

FOREVER by Evelyn Kennedy. 224 pp. Passionate romance — love
overcoming all obstacles.   ISBN 1-56280-094-9   10.95

WHISPERS by Kris Bruyer. 176 pp. Romantic ghost story
                                                        ISBN 1-56280-082-5   10.95

NIGHT SONGS by Penny Mickelbury. 224 pp. 2nd Gianna Maglione
Mystery.   ISBN 1-56280-097-3   10.95

GETTING TO THE POINT by Teresa Stores. 256 pp. Classic
southern Lesbian novel.   ISBN 1-56280-100-7   10.95

PAINTED MOON by Karin Kallmaker. 224 pp. Delicious
Kallmaker romance.   ISBN 1-56280-075-2   11.95

THE MYSTERIOUS NAIAD edited by Katherine V. Forrest &
Barbara Grier. 320 pp. Love stories by Naiad Press authors.
                                                        ISBN 1-56280-074-4   14.95

DAUGHTERS OF A CORAL DAWN by Katherine V. Forrest.
240 pp. Tenth Anniversay Edition.   ISBN 1-56280-104-X   11.95

BODY GUARD by Claire McNab. 208 pp. 6th Carol Ashton
Mystery.   ISBN 1-56280-073-6   11.95

CACTUS LOVE by Lee Lynch. 192 pp. Stories by the beloved
storyteller.   ISBN 1-56280-071-X   9.95

SECOND GUESS by Rose Beecham. 216 pp. 2nd Amanda Valentine
Mystery.   ISBN 1-56280-069-8   9.95

A RAGE OF MAIDENS by Lauren Wright Douglas. 240 pp. 6th Caitlin
Reece Mystery.   ISBN 1-56280-068-X   10.95

TRIPLE EXPOSURE by Jackie Calhoun. 224 pp. Romantic drama
involving many characters.   ISBN 1-56280-067-1   10.95

UP, UP AND AWAY by Catherine Ennis. 192 pp. Delightful
romance.   ISBN 1-56280-065-5   11.95

PERSONAL ADS by Robbi Sommers. 176 pp. Sizzling short
stories.   ISBN 1-56280-059-0   11.95

CROSSWORDS by Penny Sumner. 256 pp. 2nd Victoria Cross
Mystery.   ISBN 1-56280-064-7   9.95

SWEET CHERRY WINE by Carol Schmidt. 224 pp. A novel of
suspense.   ISBN 1-56280-063-9   9.95

CERTAIN SMILES by Dorothy Tell. 160 pp. Erotic short stories.
                                                        ISBN 1-56280-066-3   9.95

A SINGULAR SPY by Amanda K. Williams. 192 pp. 3rd
Madison McGuire Mystery.   ISBN 1-56280-008-6   8.95

THE END OF APRIL by Penny Sumner. 240 pp. 1st Victoria
Cross Mystery.   ISBN 1-56280-007-8   8.95

KISS AND TELL by Robbi Sommers. 192 pp. Scorching stories
by the author of *Pleasures*.   ISBN 1-56280-005-1   11.95

STILL WATERS by Pat Welch. 208 pp. 2nd Helen Black Mystery.
                                        ISBN 0-941483-97-5   9.95

TO LOVE AGAIN by Evelyn Kennedy. 208 pp. Wildly romantic
love story.   ISBN 0-941483-85-1   11.95

IN THE GAME by Nikki Baker. 192 pp. 1st Virginia Kelly
Mystery.   ISBN 1-56280-004-3   9.95

STRANDED by Camarin Grae. 320 pp. Entertaining, riveting
adventure.   ISBN 0-941483-99-1   9.95

THE DAUGHTERS OF ARTEMIS by Lauren Wright Douglas.
240 pp. 3rd Caitlin Reece Mystery.   ISBN 0-941483-95-9   9.95

CLEARWATER by Catherine Ennis. 176 pp. Romantic secrets
of a small Louisiana town.   ISBN 0-941483-65-7   8.95

THE HALLELUJAH MURDERS by Dorothy Tell. 176 pp. 2nd
Poppy Dillworth Mystery.   ISBN 0-941483-88-6   8.95

SECOND CHANCE by Jackie Calhoun. 256 pp. Contemporary
Lesbian lives and loves.   ISBN 0-941483-93-2   9.95

BENEDICTION by Diane Salvatore. 272 pp. Striking, contemporary romantic novel.   ISBN 0-941483-90-8   11.95

TOUCHWOOD by Karin Kallmaker. 240 pp. Loving, May/
December romance.   ISBN 0-941483-76-2   11.95

COP OUT by Claire McNab. 208 pp. 4th Carol Ashton Mystery.
                                        ISBN 0-941483-84-3   10.95

THE BEVERLY MALIBU by Katherine V. Forrest. 288 pp. 3rd
Kate Delafield Mystery.   ISBN 0-941483-48-7   11.95

THE PROVIDENCE FILE by Amanda Kyle Williams. 256 pp.
2nd Madison McGuire Mystery.   ISBN 0-941483-92-4   8.95

I LEFT MY HEART by Jaye Maiman. 320 pp. 1st Robin Miller
Mystery.   ISBN 0-941483-72-X   11.95

THE PRICE OF SALT by Patricia Highsmith (writing as Claire
Morgan). 288 pp. Classic lesbian novel, first issued in 1952 . . .
acknowledged by its author under her own, very famous, name.
                                        ISBN 1-56280-003-5   10.95

SIDE BY SIDE by Isabel Miller. 256 pp. From beloved author of
Patience and Sarah.   ISBN 0-941483-77-0   10.95

STAYING POWER: LONG TERM LESBIAN COUPLES by
Susan E. Johnson. 352 pp. Joys of coupledom. ISBN 0-941-483-75-4   14.95

SLICK by Camarin Grae. 304 pp. Exotic, erotic adventure.
ISBN 0-941483-74-6   9.95

NINTH LIFE by Lauren Wright Douglas. 256 pp. 2nd Caitlin
Reece Mystery.   ISBN 0-941483-50-9   9.95

PLAYERS by Robbi Sommers. 192 pp. Sizzling, erotic novel.
ISBN 0-941483-73-8   9.95

MURDER AT RED ROOK RANCH by Dorothy Tell. 224 pp.
1st Poppy Dillworth Mystery.   ISBN 0-941483-80-0   8.95

A ROOM FULL OF WOMEN by Elisabeth Nonas. 256 pp.
Contemporary Lesbian lives.   ISBN 0-941483-69-X   9.95

THEME FOR DIVERSE INSTRUMENTS by Jane Rule. 208 pp.
Powerful romantic lesbian stories.   ISBN 0-941483-63-0   8.95

CLUB 12 by Amanda Kyle Williams. 288 pp. Espionage thriller
featuring a lesbian agent!   ISBN 0-941483-64-9   9.95

DEATH DOWN UNDER by Claire McNab. 240 pp. 3rd Carol
Ashton Mystery.   ISBN 0-941483-39-8   10.95

MONTANA FEATHERS by Penny Hayes. 256 pp. Vivian and
Elizabeth find love in frontier Montana.   ISBN 0-941483-61-4   9.95

LIFESTYLES by Jackie Calhoun. 224 pp. Contemporary Lesbian
lives and loves.   ISBN 0-941483-57-6   10.95

MURDER BY THE BOOK by Pat Welch. 256 pp. 1st Helen
Black Mystery.   ISBN 0-941483-59-2   9.95

THERE'S SOMETHING I'VE BEEN MEANING TO TELL YOU
Ed. by Loralee MacPike. 288 pp. Gay men and lesbians coming out
to their children.   ISBN 0-941483-44-4   9.95

LIFTING BELLY by Gertrude Stein. Ed. by Rebecca Mark. 104 pp.
Erotic poetry.   ISBN 0-941483-51-7   10.95

AFTER THE FIRE by Jane Rule. 256 pp. Warm, human novel by
this incomparable author.   ISBN 0-941483-45-2   8.95

PLEASURES by Robbi Sommers. 204 pp. Unprecedented
eroticism.   ISBN 0-941483-49-5   11.95

EDGEWISE by Camarin Grae. 372 pp. Spellbinding
adventure.   ISBN 0-941483-19-3   9.95

FATAL REUNION by Claire McNab. 224 pp. 2nd Carol Ashton
Mystery.   ISBN 0-941483-40-1   10.95

IN EVERY PORT by Karin Kallmaker. 228 pp. Jessica's sexy,
adventuresome travels.   ISBN 0-941483-37-7   10.95

OF LOVE AND GLORY by Evelyn Kennedy. 192 pp. Exciting
WWII romance.   ISBN 0-941483-32-0   10.95

CLICKING STONES by Nancy Tyler Glenn. 288 pp. Love
transcending time.   ISBN 0-941483-31-2   9.95

SOUTH OF THE LINE by Catherine Ennis. 216 pp. Civil War
adventure.   ISBN 0-941483-29-0   8.95

WOMAN PLUS WOMAN by Dolores Klaich. 300 pp. Supurb
Lesbian overview.   ISBN 0-941483-28-2   9.95

THE FINER GRAIN by Denise Ohio. 216 pp. Brilliant young
college lesbian novel.   ISBN 0-941483-11-8   8.95

OSTEN'S BAY by Zenobia N. Vole. 204 pp. Sizzling adventure
romance set on Bonaire.   ISBN 0-941483-15-0   8.95

LESSONS IN MURDER by Claire McNab. 216 pp. 1st Carol Ashton
Mystery.   ISBN 0-941483-14-2   10.95

YELLOWTHROAT by Penny Hayes. 240 pp. Margarita, bandit,
kidnaps Julia.   ISBN 0-941483-10-X   8.95

SAPPHISTRY: THE BOOK OF LESBIAN SEXUALITY by
Pat Califia. 3d edition, revised. 208 pp.   ISBN 0-941483-24-X   10.95

CHERISHED LOVE by Evelyn Kennedy. 192 pp. Erotic Lesbian
love story.   ISBN 0-941483-08-8   11.95

THE SECRET IN THE BIRD by Camarin Grae. 312 pp. Striking,
psychological suspense novel.   ISBN 0-941483-05-3   8.95

TO THE LIGHTNING by Catherine Ennis. 208 pp. Romantic
Lesbian 'Robinson Crusoe' adventure.   ISBN 0-941483-06-1   8.95

DREAMS AND SWORDS by Katherine V. Forrest. 192 pp.
Romantic, erotic, imaginative stories.   ISBN 0-941483-03-7   10.95

MEMORY BOARD by Jane Rule. 336 pp. Memorable novel
about an aging Lesbian couple.   ISBN 0-941483-02-9   12.95

THE ALWAYS ANONYMOUS BEAST by Lauren Wright Douglas.
224 pp. 1st Caitlin Reece Mystery.
                                              ISBN 0-941483-04-5   8.95

MURDER AT THE NIGHTWOOD BAR by Katherine V. Forrest.
240 pp. 2nd Kate Delafield Mystery.   ISBN 0-930044-92-4   11.95

WINGED DANCER by Camarin Grae. 228 pp. Erotic Lesbian
adventure story.   ISBN 0-930044-88-6   8.95

PAZ by Camarin Grae. 336 pp. Romantic Lesbian adventurer
with the power to change the world.   ISBN 0-930044-89-4   8.95

SOUL SNATCHER by Camarin Grae. 224 pp. A puzzle, an
adventure, a mystery — Lesbian romance.   ISBN 0-930044-90-8   8.95

These are just a few of the many Naiad Press titles — we are the oldest and
largest lesbian/feminist publishing company in the world. We also offer an
enormous selection of lesbian video products. Please request a complete
catalog. We offer personal service; we encourage and welcome direct mail
orders from individuals who have limited access to bookstores carrying our
publications.